Poppies

and

Forget-me-nots

Poppies and Forget-me-nots

© copyright 2013 by Michael Jobling

ISBN 978-0-9565818-5-3

Published by Michael Jobling, trading as Treasure House Creative, Milton Keynes

Note:
The characters referred to in this novel are human and thus liable to behaviour and actions which may be common to others. However, no specific resemblance is intended to any persons alive or dead.

Contents

1. Arrival (1913)   1
2. Auntie B (1936)   5
3. Union chapel (1913)   13
4. Settling in (1913)   17
5. Who is my father? (1936)   21
6. Life in Oakdale (1913)   25
7. Prophetic insight (1914)   29
8. A prophet without honour (1914)   37
9. A house divided (1914)   51
10. Talking to Mam (1936)   65
11. Milking time (1914)   69
12. A new head (1914)   75
13. Helping Mary (1914)   83
14. A visit to Win (1914)   89
15. Plans for the summer (1936)   93
16. The end of summer (1914)   97
17. Harvest (1914)   107
18. Falling leaves (1914)   113
19. A summer's adventure (1936)   125
20. Christmas (1914)   113
21. True valour (1915)   143
22. Getting closer (1936)   149
23. A happy new year (1915)   161
24. Easter holidays (1915)   167
25. A lovely surprise (1915)   171
26. Couldn't be better (1936)   175
27. A sudden storm (1915)   181

Contents

(continued)

27. Sunday morning (1915)   194
28. Even though he die   197
29. Forget-me-nots (1915)   199
30. A surprise visit (1915)   201
31. Meeting the family (1936)   211
32. Departure (1915)   217
33. A summer wedding (1937)   221
34. Making peace (1937)   225
Postscript (today)   229

Chapter 1
August 1913

Arrival

Swirls of steam rose from between the carriages, enveloping the handful of passengers who stepped out onto the gaslit, wooden platform. Doors banged. A whistle blew. And the train began to move again, chugging away into the tunnel at the north end of the station. The Reverend James Wortley looked around, got his bearings and began to walk towards the exit, a large Gladstone bag in one hand and a leather suitcase in the other.

So here he was. After months of meetings, interviews and arranging estimates for the removal, his new life was about to begin. He felt excited, liberated —and yet anxious. He thought momentarily of his wife, Winifred. She had gone to stay with her parents while the removal took place. "I won't be able to bear it," he could hear her saying. "All that mess! all that fuss! You see to it James. I'll stay with mother and then come and organise things at the other end when the furniture arrives." Winifred would be joining him, with the boys, the day after tomorrow. For the moment, he was on his own. He missed her. It would have been nice to share this moment together. But there was no arguing with Winifred. She was one of those people who are incapable of opening their mind to the possibility that there could be any other outlook on life than their own.

James handed his ticket to the man at the barrier, who touched his forehead respectfully as he saw the clerical collar. Among the people standing in the entrance hall, James quickly recognised a man in his thirties with deep brown eyes and tightly curled, dark hair. Smiling, James stepped forward, put down his Gladstone bag and held out his hand:

"Jacob! How lovely to see you again!" he said.

"Aye, it's good to see thee an' all, Pastor," replied the man, in the local North Midlands accent. "Didst tha have a coomfortable journey?"

"Oh, not so bad, thank you. It's very good of you to come to meet me. Albert wrote to say someone would fetch me, but I wasn't sure who it would be."

Albert was the Secretary of Oakdale Union Chapel, where James was about to take up a new post as minister. Jacob was one of the deacons. James had visited Oakdale several months before to be interviewed and to "preach with a view" He remembered warming even then to Jacob Hollinshead's kind, albeit earnest, manner.

"It's no trouble," Jacob replied. "Please to coom this way, I've got 'pony and trap outside. I hope you don't mind a bit of a journey, but we decided it would be best if Mary and I took care of you tonight. We've a decent spare room and Albert had to be away from home on business—th' only thing is we live a fair step out of town."

Together, the two men walked out into the darkness. Jacob lifted James' luggage into the back of the trap and helped him up. Soon they were trotting through the dimly lit streets.

Jacob and Mary Hollinshead owned a farm a couple of miles outside Oakdale, a mile and a half along the Sheffield road and then another half mile down a long, unmetalled farm track.

Oakdale is a community of about five or six thousand people. A small river dissects the town, promoting a longstanding rivalry between the "north siders" and the "south siders" which affects every part of the town's life, finding expression in a number of sporting events at intervals during the calendar.

The other great rivalry in Oakdale, in those days at least, was between church and chapel. The tall spire of St Aelfred's church stood at the West end of the High Street, opposite the old grammar school building which dated back to Elizabethan times. There were a number of chapels of differing persuasions dotted around the town but Union Chapel was the largest—an imposing, Victorian building at the East end of the High Street, opposite the library. It was called Union chapel because it was home to a united congregation of both Congregationalists and Baptists. The two persuasions disagree only about the proper age for baptism. In a small number of locations around the country there were (and still are) chapels that affiliate to both denominations, allowing members freedom to follow their own conscience on the one issue which divides them. This was where James had been called to be the pastor. As they trotted past, he gazed up at the building with its dark, blind windows, excited at the opportunity it presented and wondering what events might take place in future days within its walls.

They turned to the left opposite the chapel, up a hill which led past the Town Hall and through the market square. The pony slowed and snorted with the exertion as they reached the summit. Eventually they came to the brow of the hill and the road sloped away downhill once more. They cantered on through open countryside, the wheels rumbling along the smooth, metalled road and then crunching, scraping and squelching along the driveway to the farm. The trap lurched disconcertingly over the potholes in the drive as they reached the last few hundred yards of the journey. Eventually, they saw a light in the distance.

"Woah, boy!" Jacob called – and they came to a halt outside the doorway of a low, stone built, thatched farmhouse. The door opened before either of the men could jump down from the trap, and the slim figure of a young woman stood silhouetted against the light in the doorway.

"How do, Mary?" Jacob called (in the local accent it came out as "our do") "Hast tha got kettle on?" He jumped down from the trap and began to unload James' bags.

The woman stepped forward and offered her hand to James. As she opened her mouth he was surprised to hear, not the local North Midlands accent, but a soft west country voice which might easily have suited a character in one of Thomas Hardy's novels. Its owner evidently came from somewhere South of Bristol.

"You must be Pastor Wortley," she said, " Do come in, you must be tired after such a long journey. Welcome to Sandybrook Farm."

✳✳✳

"That was lovely, you're a very good cook." James expressed his appreciation. It was more than politeness because the meal had indeed been excellent. He, Jacob and Mary had enjoyed it together, around the huge table in the farmhouse kitchen by the light of candles placed on the table. Electricity and gas had obviously not yet reached the farm. Jacob went out to attend to something that needed doing with one of the animals and Jacob was left alone with Mary. He tried to persuade her to allow him to help with the washing up, but she was insistent in a way that gave him the impression of a woman whose identity was totally invested in being a good hostess and housewife and who really would be offended if he insisted.

He settled for sitting by the range and keeping her company while she busied herself with the pots and pans. She moved in a graceful but purposeful way. James noticed her trim waist and the brown hair that fell in curls down her back. She had long fingers which seemed to gently caress the pots and pans. Occasionally she tossed a look over her shoulder as she spoke to him, glancing with green-grey eyes which occasionally flashed a dart of mischievous fire and then went dull as if she had quickly brought herself in check.

"I'm wondering how a lady with such a wonderful West Country accent comes to be living on a farm in Derbyshire?" he asked.

"I come from near Plymouth, originally," she explained. "My Jacob, he had a spell in the navy when he were younger. We met in a chapel down there and got married. Then, when 'is father died, we moved back up here so he could look after the farm. I'm a bit sensitive about my voice, though. People up here do make fun of the way I speak. I wish they wouldn't."

"I think the way you speak is perfectly charming" James replied, and noticed a red blush creep up her neck.

✳✳✳

The next morning, James awoke to the smell of cooking bacon and the sound of a knock on the door. He struggled to get his bearings as he woke and then heard Mary's voice, muffled, behind the door."

"I've left you a jug of hot water on the table out here, Pastor, and there's a cup of tea for you, too. Jacob's eating his breakfast downstairs, there'll be some for you whenever you're ready." James groped for his watch on the locker at the side of his bed. It was already eight o' clock—he must have slept very soundly. He hurriedly got up, washed, shaved and joined Mary and Jacob in the kitchen. Jacob had already been out milking the cows and made a lighthearted joke about the time of day and the difference in lifestyle between professional people and farmers. Three children sat around the table. Jacob introduced James to them one by one—Hannah, a sweet girl aged about nine, with enormous brown eyes and a shock of black curls, David, a mischievous young lad, a couple of years younger—almost the same age as his own boy, Matthew—and Eleanor, aged four, who was like a miniature version of her mother.

"I'll take you back into town when you're ready, Pastor," Jacob continued, "Mrs Bott, the church caretaker, will be there to let the removal men into the manse, but happen it will be after nine afore they get there, so they won't have got far before you arrive."

✳✳✳

"So, you're a navy man," James commented as he and Jacob rode back into town. "Do you ever miss life at sea?"

"Ah miss it now and then, right enough," said Jacob. "I don't miss being ordered about, and being out of sight of land for days on end. But I miss the smell of the sea and the feel of a deck under me feet. I miss the comradeship an' all."

"You've got a good life here, by the looks of things, though. Mary is a lovely woman, your children are delightful and the countryside around here is breathtaking. Does the farm do very well?"

"We make a living from it, but it's hard work. Mary and I have our ups and downs, too. I don't seem to be able to please her half the time, no matter how I try. She can be a bit moody sometimes."

James found it hard to believe that Jacob was describing the samewoman he had been talking to the evening before. But years of pastoral experience had taught him that what went on in the homes of apparently charming people behind closed doors often differed from the image of respectability they presented to the outside world—and there were always two sides to every marriage conflict. If Mary was being moody to Jacob, perhaps Jacob was doing something to provoke the reaction.

The furniture van was already outside the manse when they arrived. James set to guiding the removal men as they brought in the furniture, helping to carry small items himself. Jacob stayed and helped too. The morning sped by and by mid day James was feeling tired from the exertion. He was just going through the kitchen door with his hands full of gardening tools bound for the shed when he suddenly found himself about to collide with Mary, who was just arriving with a basket of goodies she had prepared for lunch. She looked around, "tut-tutted" at the way the men had arranged one or two things and began adding some feminine touches. By the afternoon the carpets were down, the beds were in place, most of the house was in order and there were fires in the grates.

"I'm so grateful to you both, you've been really kind —I don't know what I would have done without you," James thanked them as they set off back to the farm, leaving him alone. He had a quick wash, walked along to the Red Lion Hotel in the High Street and ordered a meal, before returning home and spending the evening unpacking and arranging the books in his study. Finally he sat by the fire and drank a cup of cocoa, staring into the flames and wondering what the next few years were going to bring. If Jacob and Mary were anything to go by, the people in this little town were kind and hospitable. He was beginning to warm to them more and more. Would Win enjoy it as well? And the boys—how would they settle down? Tomorrow they would be joining him.

Chapter 2
1936

Auntie B

It was a warm, humid, spring afternoon. Hebron chapel was packed to the doors and the air was full of a heady mixture of odours and fragrances: lavender perfume, brilliantine, tweed jackets, perspiration, melting pew varnish and flowers. Somewhere outside the chapel a cloud parted to let a ray of sunshine fall through the window onto the oak coffin that rested in front of the "big seat" where on Sunday the chapel elders would sit around the communion table.

Hywel Davies began to pump the harmonium for all he was worth as the congregation lifted their voices in the final hymn to the stirring tune of *Cwm Rhondda*,

> *Beth sydd imi mwy a wnelwyf*
> *Ag eilunod gwael y llawr?*
> *Tystio 'r wyf nad yw eu cwmni*
> *I'w gymharu a'm Iesu Mawr.*
> *O, am aros! O, am aros!*
> *Yn Ei gariad ddyddiau f'oes.*
> *Yn Ei gariad ddyddiau f'oes.*

> "What is there to give me pleasure
> In the idols of this earth?
> My Lord Jesus far outshines them

> None is equal to his worth
> Oh, to stay with him!
> Oh, to stay with him!
> In his love for evermore,
> In his love for evermore."

When the hymn came to an end, The Reverend Morgan pronounced the blessing and stepped down alongside the coffin. The undertaker walked forward, followed by a group of the deceased's male relatives who gathered round to lift her coffin and carry it to her last resting place in the village burial ground.

The family followed the coffin out of the chapel. The sister of the deceased, Louise Hughes, walked behind the coffin with her husband Tom, followed by their daughter Heulwen, a petite and curvaceous young woman with jet black hair and brown eyes. Normally her face carried an irrepressible smile but today, the smile was missing.

"I can't believe that Auntie B's dead," thought Heulwen. It had been sudden and unexpected—a fever, a few days of illness in the hospital and then she had passed away in her sleep. Auntie B had been her favourite Aunt, always full of fun, always taking an interest in her niece's achievements. Heulwen used to enjoy her Aunt's anecdotes about the children at the school where she taught in Caernarfon. Her full name was Bethan Beatrice Jones. During her childhood she had been known as "BB" to the rest of her family and over the years this in turn had been shortened to a simple "B". Auntie B's career had been the inspiration for Heulwen also to train as a teacher. She was now in the second year of her training at the Normal College in Bangor and looking forward to her first teaching practice assignment, in a village school in Anglesey.

After the burial, Auntie B's family and friends gathered back in

the chapel rooms for a meal. Although it was a sad occasion,
Heulwen enjoyed catching up with members of the family she
hadn't seen for years and being introduced to others whom she
had never met. After all the guests had gone, she helped her Mam
to wash up and tidy things away.

"Thank you, *cariad*, I couldn't have managed without you,"
Louise said as they arrived back at the farmhouse where she and
Tom lived along with Heulwen and Ieuian. Ieuian was a couple
of years younger than her. He had left school when he was 14 and
now worked as an apprentice at a garage in the next village.

"*Cariad*, I've got something important I want to discuss with
you," Louise added as Heulwen stepped towards the staircase
that led to her bedroom. "Do you have any plans for tomorrow?"

"No, replied Heulwen, though I do need to be heading back to
college as soon as I can. I don't want to miss too many lectures."

"OK, let's take time to talk tomorrow morning, then."

※※※

Heulwen sat at the big table in the kitchen, sipping a cup of tea.

"What is it, Mam?" She said, "You're looking so tense; you're
worrying me. Have I done something wrong?"

"No, *cariad*," her mother said, sitting down at the table opposite
her. "But I've something to tell you that isn't easy to say. Nor for
you to hear, I think." She paused, took a deep breath and said,

"Heulwen, I'm not your real Mam. And Tom's not your real Dad,
either. We've kept it from you all these years but we think it's
time you knew."

Heulwen looked at Louise in silence, her eyes wide with surprise. Louise continued.

"Auntie B was your real Mam," she continued. When she was young she went off to England to teach at a school there. It was in a town in the North Midlands. She did well for herself. But she took up with a man and got herself pregnant. He was already married. When she found out she came back home. Me and Tom had been trying for a child for ages and nothing had happened. There was no way she could bring the child up on her own so we offered to adopt it and take it as ours so she could go back to working as a teacher. And you were that child."

Heulwen sat, silently trying to take it in.

"You had me adopted properly—legally?" she asked.

"Yes of course. I've got a box here with your birth certificate and adoption certificate. Legally, you are ours, but biologically, Auntie B was your Mam."

"And you've cared for me as your own all these years?"

"We have and it's been a joy to us. We love you as if you really were our own. We need to tell you because Auntie B's left all her money to you in her will. We thought you'd wonder why. We thought you had a right to know."

"So far as I'm concerned, you and Dad are my real parents." Bethan said. "I love you both to bits and I always will. I loved Auntie B as well. She was very special. I can understand now why she took such an interest in me."

"She loved you too, *cariad*. It wasn't easy for her to give you up. She thought the world of you."

Chapter 3
1913

Union Chapel

D addy! we've been on a train and we had dinner in the dining car and we saw some soldiers!"

A small figure with a tousled head of fair curls threw himself along the path, talking as he ran, and leapt into James' arms. At the age of seven, Matthew was the younger of James' two sons. Edward (two years older, but with the same brown hair) smiled at his brother's enthusiasm and stood with his mother by the gate. Win was about 5' 6" high, slim, with grey eyes and wispy, mousy coloured hair, swept back into a bun. She stood, smiling and holding herself erect with her shoulders pulled back. James set Matthew down and stepped forward to greet her.

"You're early!" he said. "I was going to come and meet you at the station."

"The nine-twenty train was delayed and it was still in the platform when we got to St Pancras," Winifred explained, "so we caught it and thought we'd come and surprise you. We got a cab round from the station. It wasn't far. Everything is quite close together here, isn't it?"

"Yes, it's a lovely little town." There are some very respectable shops, and a nice park for the boys to play in, with a stream. I bet there'll be some minnows to catch, and tadpoles in the spring.

Come on in, I expect you could do with a cup of tea. The people are fine—those I've met. Jacob and Mary have been most helpful."

With that, James embraced his wife and then led them into the house.

The chapel deacons had allowed James to start with two weeks' holiday to settle in, so the next week was taken up with various jobs around the house and exploring the neighbourhood. On the Thursday they went to the cattle market, where the boys helped James to choose a pony to pull the trap which the church already provided for the minister's use. The next day they took a ride out into the countryside and had a picnic in a meadow beside a stream. Sunday came and they made their first appearance at the chapel, as members of the congregation.

A fair proportion of Oakdale's citizens attended Union chapel which had a long tradition reaching back to the 17th century. Normally about 300 adults would attend the morning service but the rumour that there would be a glimpse of the new Pastor and his family swelled the numbers so that most seats were full. A visiting preacher led the service. Afterwards the congregation responded to the newcomers in different ways. Some looked shyly from a distance with mild curiosity. Others made a point of coming up to welcome them (and get a closer look). One or two took the opportunity to lay down markers for future battles:

"We're very proud of our choral tradition here at Oakdale Chapel, I hope you'll continue to support it" (this from Miss Hall, the Choirmistress).

"We don't want any of that modernist claptrap. We want to hear about Jesus and him crucified." (from Jim Naylor, the local butcher).

A very effusive young woman with coils of jet black hair piled high on her head, an hourglass figure and an enviable complexion pushed her way through the crowd to introduce herself.

"Hello, I'm Bethan Jones," she said in a slight Welsh accent, holding out a delicate, slender hand, "I'm one of the teachers in the British School. I'm really glad to meet you, we've been looking forward for so long to having our own minister again."

"Oh yes," James observed, "I think I'm the *ex officio* chairman of the School Board, or the Management Committee I think they call it nowadays. Christian education is very important, I do intend to take an interest in the school, you can count on my support. Tell me, how many scholars do you have?"

For several minutes they talked together about the school, Bethan becoming more and more animated as she warmed to her subject, holding James' attention with her clear blue eyes. Winifred's attention wandered and she became occupied with someone else for a while but eventually became a touch jealous at the way this good-looking Welsh lady was hogging her husband's attention. She pulled on his arm and drew him away on the pretext of introducing him to someone else.

A week later, on the Saturday afternoon, the chapel was packed to the doors for the official induction service. This was when James officially took up his duties. One of James' friends from college came to preach the sermon. Officials from each of the traditions the chapel belonged to shared in leading the induction ceremony, the choir and congregation sang their hearts out. Finally, everyone went round to a large hall at the rear of the chapel for a sumptuous tea. James and Winifred's attention was once more taken up with a constant stream of people wanting their attention: relatives, old friends, people from their previous church who had come to wish them well, together with Oakdale people eager to make themselves known.

As the crowds began to move away, Winifred suddenly realised that she hadn't seen the boys for quite a long time. She finally tracked them down to the kitchen where Matthew, his face red from running about, his hair tousled and his tie no longer straight, was drinking a glass of lemonade and Edward, to her great surprise, had his hands up to his elbows in the sink and was helping with the washing up! They were both talking to Mary who seemed to be in charge of the kitchen.

"Thank you so much for all you've done!" Winifred said. "You've really done us proud. Who organised it all?"

Mary started to murmur something about it being nothing, while one of the other ladies in the kitchen began to explain that Mary, in fact, had organised the catering for the occasion, with the help of a band of willing helpers.

"My, oh my!" said Winifred, "I shall have to pick your brains. You must be a genius to bring all this together—and was it you who got my son to help with the washing up? That's a miracle! How on earth did you manage that? I can see I'll have to take some tips from you!"

"I do 'ave a family myself, Mrs Wortley," Mary explained. "I know how to get young lads to do what I want them to. A bit of kindness and a bribe works wonders. I promised him he could come over to our farm some day, have some tea and cakes and have a look at our animals. He were like putty in my hands then!"

"Well, thank you. And Mary, I know you and Jacob did a lot of work getting the manse ready for us too. I'm so grateful—and by the way, do call me Winifred. I hope we can be friends."

Chapter 4
1913

Settling in

For the first couple of months after the induction most of
James' time was taken up with getting to know people—
first his congregation, and then the circle of local
dignitaries who were his peers in the community: the mayor, the
local doctor, the rector of the parish and his two curates, the
Catholic priest, the Methodist minister, the Salvation Army
captain, the headmasters of the local Grammar school and the
British School—an elementary school that provided an education
to the children of Oakdale's chapelgoers. Once this mountain of
social visits had been scaled, he could settle into a routine.

The main responsibility of a Free Church minister was to preach
—twice on a Sunday and once during the week at the Wednesday
night Bible study meeting. The congregation expected each
sermon to be no less than 20 minutes in length, delivered
standing high above them in the large pulpit that held a central
position at the front of the chapel. The minister had to hold his
audience's attention with just his voice, his wit and an ability to
stir people's imagination through language. The content of his
main Sunday morning sermon reached a much wider audience
through a précis that appeared in the local newspaper, *The
Oakdale Gazette*, during the following week. James would spend
a considerable part of his week—often twelve hours or more—
researching material for his sermons, writing them up and

sometimes practising them under his breath.

Sermons apart, a Free Church Minister was a mixture of church manager, social worker, counsellor, therapist and a lot else. Doctors were expensive and social work as a profession hardly existed at the beginning of the 20th century. Clergy and church ministers provided the only source of free advice for most of the population. James spent a lot of time visiting or being visited, giving advice, arranging help, in a whole variety of situations ranging from unplanned pregnancy to sudden death—and everything in between.

Winifred, too, had an important, though difficult, role. Her main job was to run the house—with the aid of Ethel, a young maid who came in three mornings a week to help with the cleaning and washing. The Pastor's wife had no official role in the church and was not expected to bear any office, yet she was looked up to as a mother figure in the community. People expected her to engage in good works like her husband, as well as being part of a social circle of influential women who, like her, had no official authority but could exercise a powerful influence through the sanctions they could apply to their husbands. The Salvation Army Officer's wife might help with the preaching and bear the same rank as her husband, but that was a revolutionary idea that hadn't caught on in the community as a whole.

✳✳✳

August had drifted through into September by the time Mary's promise to Edward could be fulfilled. One Saturday afternoon the whole Wortley family drove out to Sandybrook Farm. As they approached the turning where the lane leading to the farm met the Sheffield road, they saw David, Hannah and Eleanor seated atop a dry stone wall, waiting for them to arrive. The three children waved enthusiastically as soon as James and his family came into view and then jumped down as the trap approached, running alongside it the whole half mile to the farmhouse where Mary and Jacob stepped out to meet them.

It was one of those glorious September days when the heat of summer lingers on and the countryside is bathed in golden light. The four adults took a cup of tea together in the kitchen when they arrived and the five children immediately disappeared, running around the outbuildings and finding amusement jumping from one level to another of the hay bales stacked in the barn. There is always work to do on a farm and this day was no exception. There were apples ready for picking in the orchard and blackberries to be gathered in the hedgerows. Once the adults had finished their tea everyone pitched in, the men climbing trees in the orchard and the two women and the girls walking round the hedgerows with huge baskets to gather the blackberries.

There are times in life when everything seems to go into slow motion to allow us to savour a special moment and allow it to be engraved on our memories, to be savoured again and again in the future. For James, that September afternoon was just such a moment. He would look back on it many times in years to come, remembering it as a time when life was good and filled with hope. His heart swelled with happiness. There was so much about the afternoon to savour—the special September light; the beautiful countryside; cheery conversation with Jacob who was rapidly becoming a friend as well as a colleague; the excitement and energy of the children running about the farm; the graceful figures of Winifred and Mary, who seemed set to be friends; Mary's baking—a whole selection of delicious cakes she had made for them to choose from. Everything in the world was good and beautiful that day. At the beginning of a new pastorate James felt optimistic and hopeful. Even on the political front there wasn't a cloud on the horizon. Britain ruled the waves and spread her civilising influence of Christianity, democracy and commerce throughout the world. "The empire on which the sun never sets" people said.

But eventually, the long afternoon came to an end. They said their goodbyes and "thank yous", loaded baskets of apples and blackberries and fruit cake into the trap and set off back down the rutted drive.

"What a capital day it's been!" James exclaimed. "I can't think when I've enjoyed myself so much." Edward and Matthew agreed.

"It has been enjoyable" admitted Winifred "But I pity that poor woman. Fancy living so far away from everyone. I think I would go out of my mind living out in the country like that. And with no electric light or gas! It must be a hard life for them."

As they turned onto the main road, the sun began to approach the horizon, a huge, blood-red ball which promised another sunny day tomorrow.

Darkness fell as they trotted down the hill past the marketplace and back to the house.

Chapter 5
1936

Who is my father?

C ome in!" Heulwen called. The door of her room at the Normal College opened slightly and her friend Awena poked her head around it, her head cocked to one side so that her auburn hair hung down over her shoulder. "Hi, you're back then?" she said.

"Yes, I got back yesterday evening," Heulwen answered.

"How did the funeral go? Was it very sad?"

"It was. But it was lovely to see lots of cousins that I haven't seen for years."

Heulwen hesitated and fell silent for a moment before continuing.

"I had an enormous surprise afterwards, though. You won't believe it when I tell you. I found out that my Aunty B was really my Mam. For all these years I've been adopted without realising it!"

"Never! Really? That must have been quite a shock!"

"You can say that again!" Heulwen exclaimed. "Can you come in for a while and have a cup of tea? I need to talk to someone about it."

She recounted to Awena all the details of her trip home, the funeral and then the unexpected conversation with Louise, her mother—or in fact her Aunt, as it turned out, and the feelings that she was struggling with.

"It's so confusing!" she said. "I love my Mam, she's been the best Mam I could have hoped for. She is my Mam, I can't think of her as Aunty Louise—and yet she isn't my real Mam, Aunty B is my real Mam. I'm still trying to get used to it. I feel kind of cheated that they haven't told me before, though. And yet I can understand how it came about."

"It must be very strange," Awena agreed. "And then you've got some unknown man somewhere who is your real Dad!"

Heulwen's jaw dropped. She had been so taken up with the process of reorientating her relationship with a mother who turned out to be an aunt that the question of her paternity had not entered her head.

"Gosh, yes!" she exclaimed. You know, I hadn't thought of that. I wonder who he is—and if he's still alive?"

"He could be somebody rich and famous!" Awenna exclaimed.

"Don't let your imagination run away with you," said Heulwen "But I know one thing; he must have been someone very special for Auntie B to fall for him. She had lots of admirers but she never married anyone else. I just know that the man she fell for would have to have been a man of courage and principle and someone who was gentle and kind."

"What do you know about him? Awenna asked.

"Absolutely nothing at all." Heulwen admitted. "Mam didn't say and I didn't ask." Next time I go home I'll ask Mam what she knows."

She had to wait three weeks to the end of the Spring term. Throughout the three weeks the question haunted her—who was the man that Auntie B had had the affair with? Who was her real father? Where was he, now? Would it be possible to find him? If she did, would he want her to be contacting him?

Chapter 6
1913

Life in Oakdale

The first half of 1913 had been an unsettling time of upheaval for the Wortleys. So, as the weeks sped on through September and October, it was a relief to return to some kind of normality. Although they were in a new and unfamiliar environment and had the massive task of getting to know the considerable congregation that attended the Chapel, their future was settled and they could begin to establish a daily routine. Each morning James got up early for his devotions, lit the fires and brought the rest of the family a morning cup of tea. Win then busied herself with breakfast while Jacob read the papers and began to open his post. The boys went off about nine o'clock to the British School, held in the rooms in the basement of the Chapel. James spent the morning in administrative tasks and study. Meanwhile, Win busied herself with shopping and housework.

Once a week James would take a scripture lesson in the British School. He quickly became friends with the headteacher, Albert Whale, who was also the Church Secretary. James also had some interesting and enjoyable conversations with Bethan Jones, the teacher who had caught his attention on his first Sunday at the Union Chapel. Nearly every time he met her at school or church she seemed to have an important question to ask him, usually about some aspect of theology or ethics, and she never just accepted his answers but always raised some extra question or alternative viewpoint to engage him in discussion. Invariably, she ended up by telling him how much she admired the clarity of his thinking or the depth of his knowledge and how helpful his thoughts had been. Sometimes he found her attention irritating, especially when she made him late for an appointment, but at the same time she seemed to know just how to draw him on a subject that he found really interesting and it was always pleasant to have his erudition and wisdom affirmed by someone who genuinely gave time to listen and understand—especially someone with such beautiful, expressive blue eyes and such a trim figure.

In the afternoon and evening James would visit members of the congregation or they would come to consult with him in his study at the manse. Sometimes, especially in the evening, there would be meetings for him to go to. He was the *ex officio* chairman of every committee attached to the church—the deacons, the Sunday School Teachers, the Choir, the Young Men's Group, the Boys' Brigade—even the Ladies' Bright Hour.

In the afternoons Win would also find people to call on, either visiting the less fortunate members of the congregation on errands of mercy, or calling socially on other women in the town. She soon began to develop a circle of acquaintances. Socially, a Free Church minister's wife was in a strange position. In the chapel congregation she was very much the Queen Bee—everyone looked up to her with respect. The other women cultivated her attention and she had to be careful not to make favourites in a way that would undermine her husband's position. Outside the chapel community, though, it was another story. There were three levels of society among Oakdale's women. One consisted of those who had pretentions to class or title and who could still manage a household of servants. There was another level consisting of the wives of tradespeople—owners of shops and small businesses— and then there was the mass of working people, including an army of women who were employed either full or part time in one of two large factories, the "stay works" that made ladies' undergarments and another factory that processed foods for canning.

Win was firmly excluded from the first of these three groups. This group of women counted the vicar's wife as part of their circle, though they looked down on her with a degree of pity because she could only afford one part-time housemaid. However, they viewed the wife of the chapel minister as equivalent to a tradesman's wife and so beyond the pale.

The tradesmen's wives, on the other hand, were uneasy with Winifred. They saw her as a cut above them and were afraid she would preach at them or make them feel uncomfortable by any moral stance she might take. So it was difficult to make friends. However, she began to develop a friendship with Sophia, the local doctor's wife who was the only person in the town whom she might consider as her peer. Both of them had been trained as nurses and so they had something in common.

The evenings were the worst time of day for Win, especially during the winter. James was always taken up with church business of some kind in the evenings, leaving her to sit on her own and knit, sew or read. Because of their position in society, the Pastor and his wife were expected to maintain a certain standard of living, to dress to a certain level of smartness and to entertain visitors in a particular way. They were not, however, given the means to do it. Win constantly faced frustrations with money—trying to heat the manse, clothe herself and her family and entertain all and sundry on what was actually a fairly meagre stipend. She was a woman who liked to be the centre of attention and so there were aspects of her role which she enjoyed very much. But at the same time she nursed a sense of grievance at some of the deprivations which her husband's calling subjected her to.

Chapter 7
1914

Prophetic Insight

The days turned to weeks, the weeks to months and soon Win and James had almost completed a full year in Oakdale, each season marked by its particular milestones. Harvest had its display of produce in the chapel and a harvest supper and social evening on the Saturday night; Christmas brought carol singing round the town and "carols by candlelight" with the chapel packed to the doors. Spring brought the town's annual Shrovetide football match when almost the whole community packed the streets in a no-holds-barred battle to get the large cork ball to one side of the town or the other. Then came Easter when everyone came to church in new clothes and enjoyed singing the rousing, triumphant resurrection hymns. June saw Whitsunday when all Oakdale's Sunday schools paraded through the town, the children dressed in white, before meeting together for a special service at one or other of the places of worship. A few Sundays later, Union Chapel would hold its Sunday School anniversary—a whole day of services with a musical programme performed by the children, all scrubbed clean and dressed in their very best clothes.

On the Saturday after the Sunday School Anniversary, Winifred and James had decided to hold a garden party. To the rear of the manse was a large and pleasant garden, large enough to contain a croquet lawn and a tennis court. They invited a number of guests, including Albert Whale and his wife, Jacob and Mary and their children, Doctor Edward McDonald, his wife, Sophia, and their son, Stewart.

It was a beautifully sunny, hot day. The children ran about and played tennis or croquet while the adults for the most part reclined in deck chairs, sipping lemonade or drinking cups of tea and eating sandwiches. In a very strange way, the conversation suddenly took a sinister turn that made it seem as if a cloud had crossed the sun and cast a shadow over them.

It began with a lull in the conversation and then a comment from Doctor McDonald.

"I think we must be among the luckiest people in the world", he said. "Look at us. We live in a fine little town, in one of the most beautiful parts of the greatest nation on earth. We have sandwiches to eat and lemonade to drink, the sun is shining, the world is at peace and we have the best of company. Life doesn't get any better than this."

"Amen to that! " said Albert. "These are certainly good times to live in. We have a lot to be thankful for."

"So long as we are grateful, not complacent." added James. "There's a big world out there where there is a lot of misery and poverty. Those who are at ease and prosperous are most in danger of failing to trust in God. Life is still short and uncertain. We should thank God for our blessings but not take them for granted."

"Can you not stop preaching for one afternoon. Padre?" the Doctor said, teasingly. "Keep your sermons for Sunday!"

"The pastor's right though," Mary spoke up, shyly. "We never know what might be round the corner. All kinds of disasters might happen—drought, plague, even a war."

"I don't think so," the Doctor replied. "No-one would dare attack Great Britain. Our army and our navy are so large there isn't a country on earth that would dare take us on. On top of that we have strong alliances with other nations that would come and help us. And we are a righteous, peace loving nation. We're not going to pick a fight with anyone else. So I should have thought peace was assured."

"Now that's a good example of the need to avoid complacency, as James was saying" remarked Albert Whale, sitting up in his chair and suddenly becoming animated. "Mary could be nearer the truth than any of us imagines. Let me suggest a scenario. We're not going to pick a fight with anyone. But just suppose that some other small nation in Europe—one of the Balkan countries for example—were to pick a fight over some contentious issue with a neighbouring state. What happens? They all have treaties with larger nations. Let's say the one that's attacked has a treaty with France, so they ask France to come and help them. The other might have a treaty with Germany, so they call Germany in to help them. Then suppose Germany starts to get the better of France. What does France do? They call on us to help them and our treaty with France requires us to come to their aid. Then, presto! Before you know where you are the whole of Europe is at war, dragging all the overseas colonies of each nation with them. It could happen. It could even lead to a world war!"

"Goodness me, what gruesome conversation for such a glorious day! I can't be coping with all this," exclaimed Winifred. "For goodness sake, let us think of something more pleasant to talk about!"

"A good idea!" agreed James, 'Sufficient unto the day …' as our Lord said. However, you have given me an idea for a sermon."

***

The sermon got its airing the next Sunday week. It caused a stir in
the congregation on the day, but unbeknown to James, even as he
was preaching, events were taking place which meant that its
impact would multiply even further as time went on. On the
following Thursday, when the *Gazette* printed the whole text,
rather than the usual summary, the whole town was talking
about it.

James first announced his text, which was from Isaiah
chapter 31 v 1:

> "Woe to them that go down to Egypt for help ... but they
> look not unto the Holy One of Israel."

He introduced his three headings:
1. The Egypt of self-reliance
2. The Egypt of science
3. The Egypt of political alliances,

First James talked about how easy it is to trust in our own strength
and abilities, our ability to work hard and amass a fortune and in
doing so to stop relying on God.

"We live in prosperous times", he said. "As a friend of mine was
saying all too recently, 'We live in a fine little town, in one of the
most beautiful parts of the greatest nation on earth. We have food
to eat and plenty to drink, the world is at peace and we have the
best of company.' In times like these we need to remember the
God who gave us all these blessings. It would be so easy to take it
all for granted and to begin to forget that these blessings come as
a result of obedience to God and his ways."

One or two heads in the congregation nodded in agreement.

"We live in a time when new discoveries are being made by science…" he warmed to his second point. "We hear that men have constructed flying machines. Some of us now benefit from gas and electricity to cook with. We have trains that can rush all the way to London in a matter of hours. And scientists are making discoveries about the origins of human life and about history that put things we have always believed in doubt. Some falsely suggest that Science has disproved the Bible. It may have disproved our understanding of the Bible and we may need to change it somewhat. But God's word is sure. 'Taste and see that the Lord is God' says the psalmist—an invitation to a scientific experiment. Put God to the test. Does he remove your guilt? Does he answer prayer? Does he respond when you call? Nothing can shake the faith of the man or woman who has put God to the test and found that he keeps his word."

Finally, James brought his sermon to a climax. He first acknowledged his debt to the head of the British school in drawing his attention to the fragility of the alliances which divided the powerful states of Europe into two great camps, equally balanced against one another. He likened them to the Israelites and the Jews, relying on their alliance with Egypt to protect them against the Assyrian threat. When the threat came, Egypt failed to live up to its promise. "There is no guarantee," James thundered, "that any of the nations with whom we are allied would come to our aid if we were attacked. But if any of them calls on us we could find ourselves drawn into a conflagration which could easily rage out of control and engulf the whole world. Our young men would become cannon fodder. Our young women would be left as grieving widows. Some protection these alliances give us! Our politicians appear to have forgotten that it is neither strength of arms nor strong alliances that bring security to a nation but that nation's relationship with the God who created Heaven and Earth. "Righteusness exalteth a nation" says the scripture—and righteousness is a nation's protection. Let us pray that we will neither have to call on other nations to help us, or to answer a call from them."

It was a good sermon—timely, relevant, well-delivered—and James felt a sense of quiet satisfaction as he stepped down from the pulpit and made his way to the chapel doorway to greet the congregation as they left. Many of them had been impressed by the sermon and made encouraging comments. Not everyone had found the end of the sermon to their liking, though. Some felt that James' description of the nation's young men being "cannon fodder" was alarmist and not at all the kind of thing respectable people wanted to hear about on the sabbath.

However, it was on Tuesday morning that James first began to realise the full impact of what he had said. He picked up his morning paper to read it at breakfast then suddenly dropped his toast and exclaimed, "My God...!"

"My dear, such language! What is it? It's not like you to take the Lord's name in vain!" exclaimed Winifrid.

"It's this business in Serbia—to do with the Archduke Ferdinand and his wife. I think it's going to mean a war between Austria and Serbia. Just imagine if our Prince of Wales were shot dead while visiting some foreign country. We wouldn't stand by and just let it happen. And if Austria declares war on Serbia the Russians will have to come in to support the Serbians. They have a treaty that says they have to."

"That's very dreadful dear, but I don't see how that warrants such uncharacteristically bad language" Winifred replied, reprovingly.

"Don't you see, this is exactly what Albert Whale was predicting – and what I was saying on Sunday morning. If the Russians step in to defend Serbia against Austria it's only a matter of time before Germany declares war to support Austria. They have to—they've already promised to do so in their treaty. If Germany and Russia come to blows, France will come in to support Russia and we will probably get dragged in as well.

"I'm sure the politicians will sort something out before it comes to that though," said Winifrid.

"I certainly hope you are right," agreed James.

The timeliness of James' sermon was not lost on the editor of the *Gazette*. In his editorial he drew out the link between James' sermon and the events that had occurred, almost simultaneously, in the Balkans:

"Who knows but that the stirring sermon preached this week by the new Minister of the Union Chapel may not prove to be prophetic. It is our earnest prayer that this may not be so, that peace may prevail. But should the call to arms be sounded to defend King and Country and the lands of our friends abroad, we can be sure that the brave lads of our little town would rise to the occasion."

Chapter 8
1914

A prophet without honour

The whole of Europe held its breath for a month. And then, like a house of cards collapsing, within six days, peace fell apart. A month after James' sermon, Austria declared war on Serbia. Russia mobilised its troops to come to Serbia's defence. A few days later, Germany declared war on Russia. As the congregation at Oakdale's Union Chapel gathered for worship on the first Sunday in August, France was mobilising her troops. Germany declared war on France and demanded free passage for the Imperial troops to pass through Belgium. Belgium refused. German troops crossed the border and on Tuesday, 4th August, Britain entered the war in Belgium's defence.

On Thursday, the *Oakdale Gazette* reported on these events and their probable effects on the population of the little town. The editor again referred to the sermon James had preached a month earlier.

Everyone that James met during the rest of the week seemed to have some comment to make on his alleged prophetic powers. On Friday morning James met Albert Whale outside the chapel. He was coming out of the schoolrooms in the basement where he had been catching up on some administrative work now that the term was over and all the children were on holiday.

"Well, Wortley, we weren't far wrong, were we?" He said, as soon as they met. "We saw it coming, between us."

"Not so much of the 'we', actually," said James. "As I recall you were the one that made the prediction. I just used it as the basis for a sermon."

"Well you agreed with me, James," asserted Mr Whale. "At least you didn't pooh-pooh the idea like everyone else. I wonder what things are going to be like now. Let's hope it's all over quickly. Though I don't see how it can be; the two sides are very evenly matched."

"It's certainly not going to be like any conflict we've seen in our lifetime," James observed. "War is always horrific but with the kind of weaponry around nowadays… I dread to think."

As they stood chatting, Bethan Jones also came out of the school. She was even more effusive.

"You truly must be a man of God, Mr. Wortley," she gushed, fixing him with her deep blue eyes. "You saw this terrible business coming. Nobody believed you but you stuck to your guns. We are so privileged to have a man with such wisdom and foresight in Oakdale to bring the word of God to us."

"Miss Jones, please don't build me up into something I'm not" James replied, blushing slightly and looking nervously around for an excuse to escape. "If anything I've said has been of any worth it has come from God and from other wise people I have listened to."

"But you had the courage to say it. And you always express things so well. You're a dear man. I really admire you."

James blushed and changed the subject,

"I'm surprised to see you still here after the end of term. I thought you might be going away for the summer holiday?"

"I had planned to go to Paris for a while but with all that's going on, I didn't think it was wise. Instead, I'm going back to my family in Wales for a couple of weeks – I'll be leaving on Monday. I plan to come back to Oakdale on the 24th. That will give me a couple of weeks to get ready for the new term.

"Well, I hope you have a lovely summer, whatever you do, said James."

"You too, Pastor, she replied."

"I must be getting on, said Albert Whale." "Me too, agreed James." With that, Bethan also took her leave and hurried off along the main street, away from the town.

James walked in the opposite direction, towards the centre of the little town. He cut through a passageway that led through into the market square and, as he did so, he became aware of music playing which he eventually began to identify as a military band. As the market square opened up in front of him he saw that a small contingent of soldiers was marching in the Square, to the music of a couple of cornets, a trumpet, a trombone, a tuba, two kettle drums and a bass drum. A crowd was gathering to watch. People were standing in shop doorways and open windows, enjoying the spectacle. The soldiers came to a halt and then stood at ease. A sergeant wearing a red sash turned to address the crowd. He spoke in brief, staccato phrases allowing time for the echo of his resonant voice to bounce back off the walls of the Town Hall, opposite.

"Our country—has just embarked on a war—with a pernicious enemy!" he shouted. "The Hun— thinks he can trample over

anyone's territory—without permission. We need to teach him—
to have some respect—for the British Empire. If you are capable
of bearing arms—your country needs you. Are you going to be a
coward? Or are you going to enlist? Come to the town hall now—
and volunteer—to fight for King and Country."

James' reason for going along to the market square was to visit
the post office. He intended to return to his study to tackle the
business of the morning. But, instead, his errand completed, he
walked back past the chapel, along the High Street, beyond the
soaring tower of St. Aelfred's church and out into the meadows
alongside the brook to the west of the town. His mind was in
turmoil and he needed to think. The presence of the recruiting
sergeant in the Market Square had brought him up with a start. A
war that was happening somewhere far away had suddenly come
very close. Young men from his town, from his congregation,
people he knew, were going to enlist, Some of them might be
killed. Some might be severely wounded for life. It didn't bear
thinking about. What was he going to say in this situation when he
stood in the pulpit on the coming Sunday? What solace could he
give the parents of those young men? Should he join in the call to
arms? Should he take a stand against war? Either way there would
be those who would oppose him.

Some people in the town seemed to be elevating him to the status
of a prophet because of the way his sermons had appeared to
predict the events that were taking place on the world stage. He
had the ear of the town's population at a crucial time. This was a
vital opportunity not to be missed. And yet he didn't want to
abuse the situation to fulfil his own ambitions. He didn't want to
encourage the kind of hero worship that Bethan had just been
subjecting him to. He walked along the banks of the brook for a
couple of miles or more, deep in a mixture of thought and prayer
and imaginary conversations in his mind with Winifred, with

Bethan, with the editor of the *Gazette*, with the chapel deacons and above all, with God. He returned for lunch with his mind still in a turmoil.

When he walked in through the back entrance into the manse kitchen he found Mary seated there, talking with Winifred. In response to Winifred's question about where he had been and what had detained him, he told them about the recruiting sergeant's visit to the town and how he had gone for a walk to turn over in his mind the question of his response to the war and what he should say from the pulpit the next Sunday.

He was a little startled by Winifred's response: "My darling, I do hope you're not going to make any more rash predictions. I've got so tired with everyone talking to me about it. I never know what to say. I would hate it if you stirred up any more curiosity."

"My job is to say what I think God wants me to say," he replied. "I can't alter that. People can make of it what they will, but I can't start changing my message to take account of what people are going to say about it."

"At a time like this, everyone is wanting some encouragement," Winifred continued. You have a responsibility to all those poor mothers and wives and fiancées whose men are going out to fight. They need to know that their boys are going out in a worthwhile cause.."

"But that's what worries me," James mused, "How worthwhile is it, really?"

"What do 'ee think Jesus would say?" asked Mary. "Surely, that must be your guide?"

James smiled at her kindly. "Thank you, Mary." he replied, "That confirms what I was thinking. The problem is, how to be sure what he would say. He would have been very concerned for the mothers and wives and sweethearts of our young soldiers – and for the lads themselves. But I don't think he would leave the war unchallenged." Even as he said the words a Bible verse popped into his head. "Those who live by the sword, die by the sword."

And that was James' theme when he mounted the pulpit on the second Sunday morning in August.

When he located the words in the Bible, he discovered that they were Jesus' response to Peter who had lashed out with a sword to protect Jesus from arrest and had cut off the ear of the High Priest's servant. James read out the account of the incident and Jesus' words from Matthew's gospel and then looked around at the congregation, whose faces were all turned attentively towards him. Winifred was seated about two rows back from the front, to one end of the centre row of pews. Jacob and Mary and their children were towards the back on his left. Albert and Gertrude Whale were in front, sharing a pew with Doctor McDonald and Sophia. As his gaze swept around, he became conscious of Bethan, sitting exactly in the centre of the chapel, her blue eyes fixed on him from under the rim of a large, flower-bedecked hat. It was hard not to address the sermon solely to her as her eyes seemed to hold his with enthusiastic attention. He found himself making a deliberate effort to look elsewhere.

"Peter made a great and unfortunate mistake," he began. "The results could have been tragic for the High Priest's servant, and devastating to Peter, if he had faced the rest of his life carrying another man's blood on his hands. It was a futile response and it was far from being the response that his Master expected. The King of Kings had come to fight a war. A war against evil and sin. A war to advance his kingdom. But, as Jesus himself was to say to Pontius Pilate only a few hours later—his weapons were not of this world. His was a war that would demand commitment and sacrifice and shed blood right enough but his cause was going to advance, not with the edge of the sword, not with the roar of cannon and the thunder of horse's hooves. No. His cause would advance through prayer and proclamation and acts of mercy."

James looked across and caught Mary's eye. He could see from her expression that she already guessed where his discourse was heading. She nodded and indicated her encouragement with the expression in her eyes.

"Many of us, especially the menfolk in our midst, are going to have some hard choices to make in the coming weeks and months," he continued. "There is a lot of talk about patriotism, about fighting for King and Country. It is very easy to go with the crowd, to unthinkingly do what others pressure you to do. But I ask you to pause and reflect: Who is your king? Where is your country? With whom does your true allegiance lie?" If you are a true follower of the Lord Jesus, He is your king. Heaven is your country. And Jesus calls you to a different war. He calls you just as urgently as the politicians who are today calling men to enlist in our armed forces, Jesus calls you to join forces with him. To enlist in his army. But his weapons are not the bayonet and the gun. His weapons are love and faith and preaching and prayer. Jesus warns us, 'those who live by the sword, die by the sword.' It sounds very glorious to enlist in the army or the navy and to march off to battle. But let me warn you that *that* battle is far from glorious; it is bloody and horrible and frightening and it involves death and injury and pain. Let us not be swept along by the madness of our times, but rather let us follow the footsteps of our Master.

"And let me say that I am not unaware of the terrible things now happening in Belgium. I am not justifying the German invasion. But I believe we do far more good by praying for the people there and praying that God will stop the Kaiser in his tracks than by going to fight. With that in mind I am calling for a day of prayer on Tuesday. The chapel will be open throughout the day for people to come and pray, from 6am through to midnight ..."

The immediate response to the sermon, from many of those who were present, was positive and enthusiastic.

"Well said, Wortley!" said Dr McDonald as he warmly shook James' hand at the door.

A moment later Mary stepped out into the sunlight, shielding her eyes. She caught James' eye and reached out her hand. "You're very brave." she said "I don't think everyone is going to like what you've said. But I agree with you. And it needed saying..."

"Reverend Wortley," Bethan's Welsh voice drowned out Mary's soft murmur as she barged in on their conversation, ignoring Mary. "That was wonderful! You said exactly what I've been thinking all week but far more eloquently than I could ever find the words for. Every Sunday I think. 'that man's preaching can't get any better' and then the next week you top it with something even more inspiring! Is there no limit to your wisdom and eloquence?"

James tried to play down these accolades and act modestly. And he noticed that, while Bethan monopolised his attention, there were several people who took advantage of the situation to slip quickly out without speaking to him. And some had disapproving looks on their faces.

Preaching what he expected could be a controversial sermon had drained James' emotional energy and it was a relief to finally step inside the door of the manse, to close the door and smell the pleasant fragrance of roasting beef. However, he soon realised that Winifred's reaction was very different to that of his admirers in the congregation. He stepped into the kitchen and began to engage her in small talk but soon detected a degree of distance and rigidity in her voice and manner. "Is something wrong?" he asked.

"Is something wrong? James, do you realise what you have done with that foolhardy sermon of yours this morning?"

James stood, silent, trying to think what he could have said to bring such a reaction. There was a moment of tense silence. Winifred lifted a pan from the stove and put it on the side of the range. She stood up and looked him straight in the face.

"People are going to be angry, James," she said, with a look in her eyes that suggested she was one of them. "People are looking for you to encourage them, to bring them together at a time like this, to reassure them that their husbands and sons are not going to die in vain, that we are all united in a just cause. They are looking to you to comfort them and tell them that if they do die in this war there is a Heaven to go to and if they are scared or wounded, God will be there to help them. What you said is going to make people confused and guilty. They can guess how horrible war is. At the present moment they don't want to be reminded of that. And there are going to be consequences. People are going to call you unpatriotic, James. We will be shunned by the best people in the town. Not just you, James—I will have to put up with people not wanting to talk to me and crossing over the road when I pass. And the boys, James—just think what the children at school are going to do to two little boys whose father is going to be gossiped about as a coward and a traitor."

James was surprised by the ferocity of Winifred's reaction. He could see she had a point. Perhaps, in his concern to present what he felt was a right Christian response to the situation he had been thoughtless about the possible reactions in the congregation and what they might mean for his family. But, as he tried to make Winifred understand, being a preacher meant being prepared to stand up and say unpopular things and take the consequences. "You exaggerate, my dear," he replied, "this is a free country. That's what people are fighting for, if anything. I have the right to make my opinion heard, especially when I speak, as I think I do, for our dear Lord. If people don't like what I say, we just have to put up with it. It is one of the perils of my calling. You always have been a little too concerned about people's opinions."

"Oh, you pompous hypocrite!" Winifred's eyes flashed with humiliation and anger. She went to say something, thought better of it, then said "there's never any point in arguing with you. You always think you're right. You never listen. Go away, I don't want to talk about it any more. You obviously don't care a fig for my feelings or those of your children."

The atmosphere for the rest of Sunday and Monday in the Wortley household was cold. James and Winifred avoided speaking to one another at meal times and addressed themselves only to the boys. James made one or two attempts to reach out to Winifred but met with a cold, bitter response each time.

Throughout the day of prayer on the Tuesday a constant trickle of people passed in and out of the doors of the chapel. Much of the time people sat in silence with their own thoughts and prayers. At intervals, when a larger group was present, James gathered them together into a more organised prayer meeting. There was an atmosphere of serious concern and uncertainty. People didn't know where the events on the world stage were leading. The security of their settled, country life had been shattered. Some prayed for the soldiers and sailors who were already heading off for the theatre of war. Others prayed for God to stop the madness. On Thursday the *Oakdale Gazette* carried its usual summary of the sermons preached on the Sunday morning at the parish church and the two main chapels in the town. The Vicar had told his congregation that "our brave boys" were going out to fight for a just cause, that they carried with them the prayers and thoughts of the entire town. They were marching to glory. "Whether they returned or died on the field of battle," he was reported as saying, "their names would go down in history as those who had bravely stood for the right." His real text appeared to be not from the Bible but from the Latin tag *Dulce et decorum est, pro patria mori* (it is sweet and fitting to die for one's country). He did make a passing reference to Jesus words, "greater love hath no man than this than that he lay down his life for his friends."

At the Methodist chapel a lay preacher had avoided any direct mention of the war but had addressed the issue of fear in a sermon on a verse from the Psalms "therefore we will not fear, even though the earth be removed…" However, James' sermon was the only one singled out for attention in the editorial. "In the past", wrote the editor, "we have honoured the foresight and wisdom shown by the minister of our Independent chapel. But we repudiate and abhor the cowardly and treasonable sentiments expressed in the sermon he preached on Sunday morning. Oakdale men are true to King and Country. They will not fail to support their nation in its time of need—prepared if need be to make the ultimate sacrifice. Already they are enlisting in droves. We urge those who have not yet done so and who are not hindered by ill health or duties essential to the war effort at home, to come forward and volunteer for the service of His Majesty. Those who remain at home will support them with our pride and our prayers and by taking care of the jobs they leave until they come home victorious."

At about seven o'clock on Thursday evening. James was starting to lead a Bible study meeting at the chapel. At home, Winifred and the boys were seated in the lounge. Winifred was playing the piano, Edward deeply engrossed in a book. Matthew was playing on the floor with a toy car. Suddenly, there was a crash of breaking glass, followed by a thump, and a brick slid across the polished floor, knocking the car out of Matthew's hand. Winifred stood up with a scream. Matthew shouted "Mummy!" Edward looked around, confused, then ran over to the window and pulled back the curtains. "Come away, Edward, immediately," shouted Winifred. "Traitors!" called a voice from outside. There was a sound of running footsteps. Then silence.

Shaking with shock, Winifred comforted the boys, then fetched a dustpan and brush to clear up the broken glass. James noticed the broken window as he came back later on and rushed in through the door, shouting, "Win, are you alright, what's been happening?"

"I told you this kind of thing would happen, but you wouldn't listen!" she replied, tersely, and then burst into tears with the relief of no longer being in the house on her own.

"Oh, my dear, I'm so sorry." James took her in his arms and tried to comfort her. She remained stiff and unyielding, trembling slightly still, with shock.

"Daddy, why did those people want to break our windows?" Matthew's voice broke the silence.

"I think it's because Daddy wants to stop people going to fight in the war," Edward said.

James turned towards them. "Don't be frightened," he said. "Who knows what was going through their minds. But it's over now. Thank you for being brave and looking after Mummy. You must try not to let it bother you and get yourselves ready for bed. I'll tell Constable Morris about it in the morning. I'd better try to patch up the window."

James made an attempt to temporarily board up the window while Winifred got the boys off to bed.

"James, what are you going to do?" Winifred asked as they finally got into bed together, "Well, I'll try to get the window sorted out in the morning and then, as I said, I'll catch Constable Morris on his beat and tell him what happened."

"No James, that's not what I meant," murmured Winifred. "Are you going to stop provoking this kind of reaction in your sermons?"

"Let me think about that in the morning." James replied. "Go to sleep now, if you can."

Chapter 9
1914

A house divided

James and Win sat at the dining room table for a long time after they had finished their breakfast and the boys had gone off to school. The tension between them showed in their body language. James was slouched back in his chair, his arms folded. Win turned slightly away from him, fiddling with wisps of her hair—always a sign of fear or suppressed annoyance for her.

"My dear, I have to be true to myself and what I believe." James was saying, not for the first time in the conversation. "This war is a horrible business. Young men—little more than boys—are going to die and be terribly, terribly maimed and wounded. And for what? A silly squabble between two supposedly civilised empires who ought to be able to find a better way to resolve their differences. As a Christian minister I can't stand by and just ignore it. I'm really concerned for some of our young lads who are going to enlist. If I can just make one of them think again ..."

"But what about your own boys?" Win responded, again making a point she had already made several times. "Don't you care that they are going to be scorned and persecuted and bullied at school because everyone will say their father is a coward and a traitor?"

"O come, now, Win…" James broke in, But Win kept talking. "Well, that's the way people will see it. I've already overheard people whispering things like that when I'm at the shops. James, I am deadly serious. I am not prepared to stay around here with you unless you stop this pacifist preaching of yours. I'll take the boys with me and stay at mummy and papa's until the war is over and things settle down."

As she said those words there was a knock at the door and Ethel, the maid, came in. "Excuse me Sir and Ma'm," she said. "This letter's just been delivered for the Reverend Wortley."

James took the letter, tore open the envelope and began to read it. It was from Mr Naylor, the butcher. It was to express his anger at the stance that James had been making in his preaching against the war. A minister had no business to be meddling with politics, he said. James should restrict himself to preaching the gospel. In a situation where hundreds of people might be going to a Christless eternity, James's priority should be to urge on people the necessity of getting put right with their Maker and preparing to face the judgement to come.

James read it and pushed it across the table to Win, gesturing for her to read it. She glanced over the lines and then looked reproachfully at James and said "Doesn't that just illustrate my point. Perhaps you should pay some attention to him."

✳✳✳

Sunday came round again. James intended to avoid controversy this week by preaching from a comforting text in Isaiah and avoiding any mention of the war. But as he stood in the pulpit on the Sunday morning and began to read out the scripture passage he was planning to preach on, the door at the back of the chapel opened and a group of four or five ladies entered. They began to walk up the aisle to James' right. He recognised them as people he had seen in the town but not part of his regular congregation. He followed them with his eyes, continuing to read but momentarily losing his place. He looked down, found the next sentence, started to read it and then faltered again as he looked up and realised that, rather than looking for a seat in the congregation, they were continuing right up to the front.

"Can I help you?" James asked, politely. One of the women detached herself from the rest of the group and walked up the steps into the pulpit. She lifted her hand and James looked down to see she was holding out to him a white feather. She began to speak.

"In these days," she began, "our country needs men of courage, not cowards and traitors. This white feather marks you out as a coward. We are giving it to any men in our community who will not enlist for the war to shame them into doing their duty. We are starting with you because, not only are you not going to fight to protect the families in this town, you are encouraging other men to be cowards too. Shame on you, sir!"

She then pushed the feather into the top pocket of his jacket, took a step back and then slapped him across the face with the back of her hand. She rejoined her companions and then the group walked out of the chapel. Most of the congregation sat in stunned silence. A few muttered amongst themselves or said "Shame!" quite loudly as the women passed them.

As the door closed behind them, James began to speak.

"Well, Jesus tells us to present the other cheek and he warned us that we would be reviled for following him." he said. "Those ladies have a right to their opinion, though I think not to the way they expressed it. I have a right to my opinion and I stand by all I have said from this pulpit over the last few days." Then he continued with the service.

Although he retained his composure, this incident disturbed and
unsettled him, especially when he added it to Jim Naylor's letter
and the brick thrown through the window only a few days before.
He felt fragile and vulnerable as he returned home. He longed for
Win to console him, to reassure him of her support. Instead, her
silence and her general demeanour proclaimed all too clearly that
she was still feeling angry—whether with him or with the ladies
who had intruded on the service, he could not tell and dare not
ask. They ate in silence. At one point Matthew started to say
something about "those ladies…" but he was forestalled by a kick
under the table from Edward, who also caught his eye and shook
his head vigourously in a warning gesture. After dinner, James
withdrew to his study and paced up and down, turning the
situation over and over in his mind and trying to direct his
thoughts to God in prayer. Towards the end of the afternoon the
doorbell rang and he heard voices in the hallway. Win came and
knocked at the study door. "James, Albert Whale is in the hall, he
would like to see you," she said. James urged her to show Albert
in. He guessed that he had come to encourage him or to pass some
opinion on the events of the morning. It would be good to have
someone to talk to about it. He respected Albert's integrity and
intelligence. Just the person he needed at a time like this.

"Come in, Albert, I'm so glad to see you," he said enthusiastically
as he stepped into the hallway to meet him. He quickly ushered
the school head into the study and sat him down in one of the
armchairs that stood either side of the French windows. "Can I get
you something to drink?" he asked, hospitably. "No, thank you
James," Albert replied, "I don't want to keep you, I know
Sunday's a busy day for you and you probably still have things to
sort out for the evening service. No, there's something important I
need to tell you. I didn't feel it was right to raise it this morning
after all that commotion with the ladies. I hope that didn't get to

you, by the way—just a bunch of over-zealous, emotional women in my view. There wasn't any need for it. We all have a right to our opinions and we should respect other people's—as I respect yours, dear boy. There was no call for them to intrude on divine service like that. It was very irreverent and, as I say, disrespectful. But, James, I hope you will respect my opinions in return because I have a feeling you may not be too happy with what I'm going to tell you. To cut it short, James, I'm enlisting. I'm a former soldier. I did my bit against the Boers and it seems to me this business is much more serious. Young men that I've taught over the last few years are going to be called up and I just couldn't cope with the knowledge of them putting their lives at risk for King and Country while I stayed back at home. As a figure of influence in the community, people are going to look to me to set an example. I've been in touch with my old regiment already and I will be off as soon as we can make temporary arrangements for the school to function without me."

Albert took an envelope from inside the pocket of his jacket and handed it over to James. "As you are the chairman of the school management committee, I am giving a letter of notice to you. I'm not sure if this should be a resignation or a request for leave of absence. I would like to hope that my job might be open for me if and when the war is over and if and when I return, but I understand that could create problems and I'll leave it to the school managers to decide how to play it."

Albert fell silent. The silence filled the room. James searched frantically for the right words. There were so many things he wanted to say. So few words to say them in. He wanted to say how disappointed he was. How at that moment he needed Albert's friendship, his advice. He wanted to say how he felt let down, how hurt he was that his preaching over the last few Sundays had not persuaded Albert to take a different view, to set a different example. He wanted to say how much he would miss

Albert's presence and friendship, how worried he was about how the school would fare without him. He wanted to express his admiration of Albert's bravery, to say that he wanted to still be friends even though they held a different outlook.

"What can I say?" he ventured, tentatively. He managed to express some of what was on his heart. Above all he assured Albert of his constant prayers for his safety and said a prayer for him there and then. As Albert got up to go, James held his hand longer than usual in a warm, firm handshake. "God be with you!" he said. "And with you, friend," Albert replied. This town will need someone like you to comfort people and to be there for them when the dead and wounded start coming back from the front. Your stand is courageous too and you will be in my prayers."

With that, Albert left. James sank back into the chair in his study. "Oh, God, where will it end?" he groaned out loud as he opened the envelope.

❋❋❋

James entered his study on Monday morning with a heavy heart. He had a sense of foreboding, partly arising from the animosity that his stand was attracting from people in the community, and partly coming from the awareness that it was up to him as chairman of the management committee to get all the members together to decide what they would do to replace Albert in his position as Headmaster.

James seated himself in the same armchair he had sat in the day before as he met with Albert. He opened a Bible on his lap and tried to proceed with his usual morning devotions. There was a knock at the door and Winifred entered. To begin with he assumed she was bringing a message or announcing the arrival of a visitor.

Instead, she sat opposite him, in the chair that Albert had occupied the previous afternoon.

"James, I have something to say," she began. "Please hear me out before you respond. I am not prepared to see the boys having to cope with the situation we are in. I don't agree with the example you are giving them, but it's more than that. As I've said before, they are going to get humiliated and insulted and bullied at school because of you and, I don't even think it is safe for them to stay in this house. We've had bricks through the window – what if some fanatical person decides to set fire to the place?"

"One brick…" James corrected her. It was not a wise interruption; the effect on Winifred's anger was like pouring paraffin on a fire.

"James, for goodness sake, I asked you to hear me out, now please don't interrupt again until I have finished." She stood up as she spoke, her eyes flashing, "I am asking you one more time to reconsider this pacifist nonsense and to show some care and compassion for the effect it's having on your family. If you will not change your tune, I am going to take the boys and go home to mother and stay there until things change. This is the last time I am going to ask you."

She stopped talking. James sat in silence for a while.

"Have you finished?" he asked, eventually.

"Yes. But have you?" Winifred replied.

"Win, I know this is really hard for you and the boys," James said, thoughtfully, looking down at the carpet to begin with. He raised his eyes to look into Winifred's as he continued "But I have to be true to myself. I can't live a lie. And I believe that the example I am setting to the boys is the best. I am standing by what I believe is true. I want them to grow up to do the same."

"That sounds so spiritual!" Winifred spat out the words, her voice shaking slightly. "I believe you love yourself more than you love Edward and Matthew and me."

"I don't think that's fair," said James. "I love all three of you deeply. But I can see the wisdom in taking the boys out of the situation. I won't object if you do as you say. I shall miss you all terribly. I wish you would stay, but I shall understand if you feel this is the only way."

The conciliatory tone in his voice took some of the steam from Winifred's pent up anger. "I wish you wouldn't be so pig headed, James," she said, more calmly. "I'll send a telegram to mother and make the arrangements." James reached out to take her hand as she turned to leave, but she pulled it away.

✳✳✳

During the next few days James kept hearing of one after another of the men in the congregation who were being called up or were volunteering to go to war. Some were just boys—young lads in the chapel Boys Brigade Company, even. Each time that he heard of another volunteer, James' heart grew heavier. He found it hard to relate to the "gung ho" enthusiasm that shone in so many of their eyes. He had a number of conversations with mothers and wives as well. Some of them were distraught and scared of what the future might hold for them and the men in their lives. It was easy to deal with the tears—a touch on the arm, a reassuring word about God's protection, a gentle prayer. It was draining, but also fulfilling. It was part of what he'd been called to and prepared himself for as a Christian minister. But it was the pride that he found most difficult to handle. The women who boasted of their man "doing his bit for King and country" and those who enthused about how fine they looked in their uniforms. These men and boys were going out to kill other young men and boys of their own age who came from another avowedly Christian country and looked to the same God to protect them and side with their cause. Worse still, some of them would be killed. And it was he, James, who would have to speak at the funerals and say something to comfort those same women.

All of the conversations James had with the families were difficult. But one of the most difficult took place on Wednesday morning of the same week. Like the meeting with Albert it came out of the blue. James had just entered his study to start his day's work and was opening his correspondence when he heard the doorbell ring and the housemaid ushered Jacob into the room. James had developed a warm affection for both Jacob and Mary, ever since his first day in Oakdale. Here were two people that he felt he could trust and be himself with. He never felt criticised by them, never felt the need to be careful of what he said when they were around. They were warm, friendly and hospitable, understanding and supportive and always ready to give careful consideration to any idea of James' that was new to them, even if it challenged thoughts or beliefs they already held. He instinctively sensed that they were discreet and that he could trust them with his deepest thoughts and feelings without fear of them saying anything harmful in the wrong place. They were simply a thoroughly nice couple.

"I've made a big decision, Pastor" Jacob began. "I'm going back to sea. I've to report to the Naval barracks at Portsmouth next Monday."

"O, Jacob!" James exclaimed. There was no way he could hide his distress. He assured Jacob that he would be sorely missed, tried to remonstrate with him, to urge on him his own pacifist

principles. But Jacob was repectfully determined. "This is
something I have to do, Pastor." he said, "for my King
and Country."

"But isn't Jesus your King?" James retorted. He bit his lip as
Jacob's face began to show distress. It was obvious that Jacob
didn't want to fall out with James and, for his part, James didn't
want to put him under pressure.

He reached out and touched Jacob on the arm as he quickly said,
"Jacob, I must respect your principles as I hope you respect mine.
You are a dear friend and, if you really believe that this is what
you must do, believe me when I say that my thoughts and prayers
for a safe return will go with you, even though I regret the step
that you are taking." He hesitated and then gave expression to
another doubt in his mind.

"What will Mary do?"

"I were cooming to that, Pastor" Jacob continued." She's going to
try to run the farm on her own. We've been in touch with a couple
of older hands who won't be going to war. They'll coom in and do
few hours a week—and the children will do their bit an' all. But I
were wanting to ask a special favour of you, like. I were
wondering if you could pop in once a week or so to make sure
she's alright and to keep an eye on her and to try to help her
organise extra help if she should need it. It will be a great comfort
to me to know that you're looking out for her and the lad and the
lasses until I coom back."

"Jacob, I understand what you are saying and I take it as a sacred
trust. I will watch over Mary for you and if there is ever any time
that she is in need I will be there to give her my support, you can
count on me for that."

For the rest of the day, James found it impossible to work. His mind kept turning over the terrible consequences of the war. One moment he was thinking of the rift that had grown between him and Win and how lonely it would be without her and the boys around him. Then he was thinking about the school and how it was going to survive without Albert's leadership. Then he was thinking about Mary having to run the farm on her own. And then his mind wandered over all the conversations he had had over the past week with young men who were preparing to go to war or with those they were leaving behind. Then his thoughts would turn back to him and Win again and so on.

On Thursday morning he took Win and the boys to the station. There was a strained, unpleasant atmosphere between them. He and Win tried to be positive on behalf of the boys. He tried to be caring and attentive towards her. But she seemed cold and distant. Both of them were feeling hurt while suppressing their feelings. The boys were not their usual cheerful selves either. Matthew misbehaved all the way to the station. Edward was reserved and serious apart from telling Matthew off and starting an argument between them. Matthew burst into tears as the train drew into the platform and had to be physically lifted into the carriage screaming and complaining that he didn't want to leave his Daddy. Win closed the window and sat down as soon as the train began to move, rather than standing and waving as she would normally have done in such circumstances. Even so, James stood and waved as the train disappeared round the bend. Then he turned and, with a tear trickling from his eye, he wearily walked along the wooden platform, over the footbridge and then out through the ticket office to where his pony and trap were waiting.

What with the tension between him and Winifred and the preparations for her departure with the boys there had been little time for James to concentrate on preparing for Sunday. He found it difficult to put his mind to it now although, at the same time, trying to put his mind to it helped him to cope. He decided to avoid controversy this Sunday. He was well aware of the anxiety and emotional pain that many in the congregation would be going through as they said goodbye to loved ones. Winifred was not leaving him to face the horrors of the battlefield, but her departure helped him identify with how some of the wives and mothers must be feeling.

What comfort could he bring? He took his Bible and laid it on his study desk. It fell open at a chapter familiar from many Christmastime carol services, Isaiah chapter 9:

"The people walking in darkness have seen a great light…"

✳✳✳

Sunday was a difficult day. James felt desperately alone without Win there. The house felt empty and bleak and, as he stood in the pulpit, he was desperately aware of the empty pew where Win normally would be sitting with the two boys beside her. There were other empty pews as well. Albert Whale had gone. And there were many other men, young and old, who were missing as well as one or two of the women who had enrolled as nurses. He tried to exude comfort and confidence but it was superficial. Something within him was numb. After the service he stood at the door as usual to say goodbye to people as they left. A few people noticed Win's absence and enquired after her. He tried evasively to shrug off her absence as just a brief visit to her parents.

Jacob and Mary and their children were among the last to leave. James hailed Jacob warmly and said "Tell me, what time do you plan to leave tomorrow, I'd like to come and see you off".
"I s'all have to catch the six thirty train, Pastor" he said. "I were going to ask you a favour as it 'appens."

"Ask away", James replied

"I don't want to drag Mary and the bairns all the way into town with the pony and trap, and then for them to traipse all the way back on their own after. I were wondering if I could leave the trap with thee, and then thee take it back later."

"No problem at all, Jacob," James looked him straight in the eye with warmth and compassion. And no need to bring it to me first. I shall meet you at the station about 6.15. You and Mary can say your goodbyes in private at home and Mary will know that you've got a friendly face to wave goodbye to when you catch the train."

Chapter 10
1936

Talking to Mam

Eventually, the Easter vacation arrived. Heulwen's journey home to Hebron village was short but convoluted. It involved a bus to Caernarfon, another bus down the coast, and then a journey into the mountains on a narrow gauge railway.

Mam was concerned to know how Heulwen was coping with what she had shared with her after Auntie B's funeral and raised the subject the following day. That gave Heulwen a natural opportunity to ask the question that she had been turning over in her mind.

"I've been wondering, Mam. It didn't dawn on me to start with but eventually the penny dropped that there is, or was, a man who is my father—some man who has a daughter he doesn't know anything about. I've been wondering about it for the last three weeks: Who is he? Where is he? Would he be pleased to see me if I tracked him down? Is he someone I would feel proud of—or ashamed of? Tell me, Mam, please be honest, do you know anything about him? What can you tell me?"

"I'm sorry, *Cariad*, I'm as much in the dark as you are," was the response. "Your Auntie B refused to tell us anything about him. It wasn't for lack of asking, you know. I pretty well gave her the third degree but she wouldn't crack. The only thing I know is that he was a gentleman who had a position of respect in society. That's one of the reasons why she came back home, so as to avoid there being a scandal. As soon as she found she was pregnant she left and came home and didn't have any more to do with him."

"And where was it she was living when she met him?"

"It was a town in England called Oakdale, in the North Midlands. She was a teacher in a school there. In fact when the Great War started, the Headteacher went off to war and Bethan stepped into his shoes and was running the place."

"Hang on!" Louise added, suddenly. "I found something in Auntie B's possessions that might give a clue."

She went upstairs and re-appeared a good ten minutes later, after some rummaging. In her hand she held a small, faded piece of notepaper. Heulwen took it and started to decipher the handwriting."

"My dear Bethan,

I am so ashamed about what has happened. I despise myself for my weakness. I should have behaved more responsibly. Please understand that nothing of the kind must ever happen again. At the same time I would like to assure you that, however wrong it was, I cannot remember it with anything but joy and gratitude. I shall always cherish the memory of those precious moments and you will always have a special place in my heart. I am, as you will realise, in your power. You now have the wherewithal to destroy my life. Please look kindly on my plea to be discreet and spare me the terrible consequences should what passed between us be widely known—consequences that would also not be pleasant for you. Let us try to be strong and act responsibly when we see each other again.

With fondest regards from James."

"That's got to be him!" Heulwen exclaimed. "Why else would she have kept his letter all these years?"

—

Chapter 11
1914

Milking time

Jacob was not the only man going off to war that morning. The wooden platform of Oakdale station was crowded with young men and their families—some already in uniform, others still in civvies but heading off to join a regiment or, as in Jacob's case, to report to a ship or a naval shorebase. Jacob once again reinforced his request for James to keep an eye on Mary. Once the train had pulled away and disappeared round the bend, under the footbridge and out of sight, James lingered to talk to and comfort three or four different families who had said goodbye to young men going off to war.

The station forecourt was almost empty by the time he emerged, unhitched Jacob's pony and climbed into the trap. He trotted round the corner to the manse, intending to grab a spot of breakfast, but on the way he thought of how Mary must be feeling and decided to take the pony and trap straight back to the farm. He paused just long enough to load his bicycle onto the back, where Jacob's luggage had been, and then headed straight off, through the town, up Market Hill and out along the Sheffield road.

Hannah opened the door when he knocked. "Mummy's milking the cows, she said". He replied, "Don't worry my dear, I'll go and find her" and walked round the corner into the farmyard and across to the milking parlour. To begin with, as he stepped through the doorway, he could only see the steaming backs of the cows.

"Mary?" he called.

Her head poked up above one of the stalls, her hair dishevelled, one long lock hanging down over her left eye. She brushed it away and greeted him,

"Hello, Pastor."

"I've brought the trap back," he said. "Jacob caught his train with no trouble and it left on time." He hesitated and then added, "You must be feeling very sad."

"I shed some tears," she agreed, "no doubt I'll shed some more in time."

"Would you like some company for a while?" he asked.

"That would be nice," she said, "but I must get these cows milked first. Would 'ee like to go and make yourself at home in the kitchen and I'll join you when I'm done."

"Can I not help you?" he asked.

"Have 'ee ever milked a cow before?" She smiled.

"Well, no. But I could learn. If you wouldn't mind teaching me!" He laughed.

He stood and watched as she milked the next one. "Now you try," she said.

Gingerly, James took two of the udders in his hand and tried to squeeze and pull as Mary had shown him. Nothing seemed to happen.

"Let me show you again," she said and changed places with him. The milk spurted into the pail as she showed him a second time. Once more he took over. This time he managed to produce a small trickle.

"That's a little better, you be getting the idea," she said. "But 'twill take you forever at that rate. You need to be firmer.'Twill be best if I show you the way I was taught—but you must excuse me getting closer to you than you might find comfortable." She came and crouched alongside him as he sat on the stool and reached over, in front of him, putting her hands on the cow's udders. "Now put your hands over mine." He could feel her hair tickling the side of his face and the softness of her breast pressing against his upper arm. Obediently, he placed his hands over hers. She began to squeeze and pull with a firm, rhythmic movement. Again the milk spurted into the pail. "Follow the movement of my hands with yours," she said. He obeyed. After a minute or so, she stopped and said "Now, you do it and I'll put my hands over yours. He did as she asked. It felt very pleasant, he thought to himself, feeling her hands gently closing over his. This time it worked and the milk began to flow.

"I've got it!" he exclaimed. "That's splendid!"

"Well done!" she smiled and released her hands. "Now keep going."

Soon, he was able to milk on his own, without supervision.

"It gets done a deal quicker with two of us working together!" Mary said when they'd finished, "come into the kitchen and I'll fix us both a nice cup of tea."

They sat, either side of the scrubbed, oak table, sipping from the cups they cradled in their cold hands to warm them up.

"How do you feel about Jacob going back to sea?" James asked.

"I feel torn apart." Mary responded, after a pause. "I hate him going. I think this war is madness. As a farmer he don't have to go —but he wants to be loyal to his king and country. He would feel restless and a coward if he stayed. But I have to respect his wishes. I promised to obey him when we were wed, so I must do as he says. But the farm needs him. The kiddies need him. And I need him too. And I am so scared that… that…

She was unable to complete the sentence as the tears welled up in her eyes and a sob rose in her throat. James reached across the table and gently touched her arm. What could he say? He said nothing.

Mary wept, silently for a moment, then turned her face towards the window and gazed at the distant hilltops while she pulled herself together.

"Look at me," she said. "I'm not the only lonely one around here. There's plenty more women in the same situation. And you're having to fend for yourself without Win at the moment from what I hear?"

"Yes, indeed," he replied.

"How long has she gone for?"

"I'm not sure," said James, evasively.

"I hope you don't mind me saying, but she hasn't seemed happy recently." Mary probed.

"Well, yes," agreed James, "To tell the truth, we haven't exactly been seeing eye to eye where the war is concerned. A lot of people in the town are hostile to the stance I've taken in some of my sermons and she didn't agree with me. She was worried about the boys being bullied because of me and decided to take them out of it."

"Well. I for one think you are right. And I think your boys should be proud to have such a brave father. And what if they are bullied, if they have your example to inspire them? Better to be bullied than shot to pieces on the battlefield." Mary flushed slightly as she spoke.

"That's very kind of you to say so, Mary," James responded. But I can understand Win's point of view."

After half an hour or so, James got up from the table to go.

"Thank you for your company, Pastor," Mary said, "and for helping with the milking."

"I enjoyed it," James said. "Would you like me to come and help you again? There must be other things that need doing around the farm as well—not just the milking."

"Well, I don't know …," Mary hesitated. "There must be lots of other people that need your help as much as me …"

"None that are trying to run a farm on their own," James observed, "and I promised Jacob that I would look after you."

Mary looked up and met James's eyes as she responded,

"Well, Pastor, you be always welcome here. Let me say no more than that."

Her eyes said, "please come".

"Expect me on Friday morning—in time for the milking", he said.

Chapter 12
1914

A new head

James sat in his study the following morning with his Bible
on his knees, praying and again trying to get some order into
his mind. Everything was happening so quickly. Less than a
month before, life in Oakdale had been following its regular,
sleepy routine. Within a matter of weeks everything had been
turned upside down. Win had gone off to her mother and father's
home and taken the boys with her. Half the men in the town had
either gone to war or were making preparations to go. Half of the
deacons of Union chapel had gone to join the forces, including
Jacob, the reliable treasurer and Albert Whale, the secretary. With
Albert's departure, the nonconformist school was also without a
head teacher. He would need to take action to get all of those
vacancies filled.

By chance a meeting of the school management committee was
due on Wednesday evening—he would arrange for the
headmaster's vacancy to be on the agenda. And he would need to
call a meeting of church members.

His prayers over, he decided to take a walk along the main street
to buy a newspaper and a few toiletries that he needed—things
Win would normally purchase if she were at home.

All along the street little groups, mainly of women, stood around talking earnestly. There was a strange atmosphere in the town – tense and anxious, the opposite of the excitement that had been in the air two weeks before when the recruiting sergeant had made his visit to the market square. James stopped to talk to one or two people that he knew. Everyone had at least one man in their family or circle of friends who had gone off to war and was concerned about what would happen to them. Where were they? Had they gone to the front yet? When would news of them come? He tried to be positive and encouraging, helping people to lean on their faith and encouraging them to pray, but in his heart he knew that the time would come only too soon when young men would begin to return with injuries or, worse still, would be reported as killed in action.

Arriving back at the manse, he decided to write to Win. He made several attempts at composing a letter, expressing the loneliness he felt but, in the end, he decided to go and see her the following Monday and simply wrote a letter to let her know his plans and the time he expected to arrive.

The week dragged by. He kept being brought up short by things that Win normally would attend to that now he had to deal with himself. Ethel continued to come and do the cleaning and cook the midday meal as before but, in the evenings, he had to prepare a meal for himself. He filled the time with his usual duties of sermon preparation, correspondence and visiting. With so many menfolk away he found himself volunteering to do little chores for women whose husbands or sons had gone to war—bringing in some coal for Mrs Bentley, mending a leaking toilet for Mrs Allsopp, trimming a hedge for Mrs. Shotton.

On Wednesday evening he chaired the school management committee meeting. The numbers were depleted and the first item on the agenda was appointing new members to replace those who had gone to war. The Methodist Minister, Frank Singer, was there, attending his last meeting before going off to be an army chaplain. A couple of influential ladies from the town were the only two other members present. Having made a list of people who might be approached to take the vacancies on the committee, they turned their attention to the question of the vacant headship.

"Even if you advertise, you'll have a job to find someone," observed Frank Singer. "All the best men have gone off to fight. You might find a retired teacher who's prepared to come back. Or someone whose health isn't up to scratch. But in my opinion that would be giving the children second best."

"What about the staff we already have?" asked Sophia McDonald, the Doctor's wife. "Would we not be better off appointing someone who already knows the school and the children? I was thinking of Miss Jones. She is such a good teacher, the children love her and she has been at the school a good three years now. I believe she has the drive and enthusiasm to lead the school and to do a good job."

"Would the other staff accept her leadership?" asked James.

"I believe she is well thought of by the other teachers." observed Mrs. Stafford, the other member of the committee present, "And I believe she has the enthusiasm and confidence to carry it off."

"I've no doubt she has," thought James to himself. He was aware that Miss Jones could be quite overpowering and determined. He had a strange mixture of emotions about the idea. On the one hand he knew that she could be hard to withstand—she was a young woman who rarely took "no" for an answer. As he was the Chair of the management committee, she would be directly answerable to him. They would have to spend time together discussing school matters. The thought of meeting with her

regularly was not unpleasant—therein lay a problem. The idea of
her taking on the role of headmistress touched on a fear of his
own reactions to her. He frequently found her conversation
stimulating. She was bright, intelligent and witty—and then there
were those curling black locks and her soft, white complexion. He
realised he would enjoy regular meetings with her and wondered
if he might enjoy them too much. He came up with several
reasons why appointing her might not be the best move but the
other three committee members came forward with convincing
counter-arguments. In the end, he was obliged to go along with
them and they took a decision to offer the headship to Miss
Bethan Jones.

James remembered that Bethan had intended to arrive back in
Oakdale on 24th August. He needed to inform her of the
management committee's offer as soon as possible. She lived in a
cottage on the edge of town, on the Manchester Road. He would
have to go and visit her. It was unusual for a gentleman to call on
a single lady unannounced and without an appointment but there
was no way round it. He timed his visit for the middle of
the morning.

The front door of the cottage was painted white and pale blue,
with a small, stained glass window above the letterbox. White
painted trellis work formed a porch around the door over which
red and yellow rambling roses climbed. James knocked at the
door a couple of times but there was no answer. He stood on the
doorstep for a moment, feeling in his pockets for a pencil and a
scrap of paper to leave a note asking her to contact him. Suddenly
someone crept up behind him and covered his eyes with a pair of
gloved hands,

"Guess who?" There was no doubting the voice.

"Miss Jones," He said, "You gave me a fright!"

"You too, Pastor. I thought I had a burglar until I realised it was you. I've just been for a little walk to get some fresh air. But it's a pleasant surprise to find you standing at my door. To what do I owe the honour?"

"I have a proposition …" he began, then realised the word might be misconstrued and started again, "I have something important to tell you. I wonder if I might come in to talk to you for a moment or two, it's not something I can say in a few minutes."

"Curiouser and curiouser!" Bethan exclaimed, widening her eyes. "Fortunately I tidied up before I went out. Do come in. Can I offer you a cup of tea or coffee?"

"Perhaps in a moment," he said, "But let me get this matter off my chest first."

They stepped into the front room of the cottage, where the blue and white theme continued into the fabric of the sofa and armchairs and the paper on the walls. The sun streamed in through a window in front of which stood an aspidistra in a large, brass pot. Bethan sat on the sofa and patted the seat beside her to invite him to sit. Instead he remained standing,

"I've come to see you on behalf of the School Management Committee, with a very special message…" he began,

"Goodness, I hope I've done nothing wrong!" Bethan exclaimed, a flash of genuine anxiety showing in her eyes.

"We had a meeting of the Management Committee last night to talk about the vacant headship. Normally, of course, we would be looking for a headmaster but so many male teachers have gone off to fight and we don't want to leave the school without direction for too long. The suggestion was made that an admirable solution would be to appoint you as Headmistress. The idea met with a very positive response and I am here on behalf of the Committee to offer you the job. This would, of course, only be a temporary arrangement for the duration of the hostilities. In the event that hostilities cease and the Good Lord preserves our dear Mr Whale and brings him safe home, he would of course resume his position. But in the meantime you would be in charge. We propose that you reduce your teaching hours by half to make way for the extra duties of headship. Assuming you accept the position, we will then discuss with you what arrangements we can make to cover those extra hours—whether to employ another teacher part time or perhaps even for me to come in to take a few lessons.

"So, I'm offering you the job. What do you say?"

For a full thirty seconds, Bethan said nothing. And then,

"Goodness!" Followed by another long silence. Then

"I don't know what to say, I'm honoured! What an opportunity! Well, yes, I accept!"

"I'm sure you'll make a wonderful job of it!" James said, smiling. Bethan too stood up and looked at him with excitement and pleasure shining in her clear blue eyes.

"I'm so amazed!" she said, "I thought for a moment you had come to reprimand me about something. But this is so thrilling. I'm overwhelmed. Thank you, I feel I could hug you!"

"That wouldn't be appropriate," James said firmly. "Perhaps that cup of tea would be an appropriate way to show your gratitude?"

Having delivered his message, he sat down in an armchair by the fireplace. Bethan came back with a tray a few minutes later. They discussed how the staff timetable could be rearranged to accommodate the change. James proposed calling a special staff meeting during the following week to announce the appointment.

Having drunk the tea, James took his leave. He turned to wave as he opened the garden gate. Bethan was standing at the door, her eyes gleaming with excitement. "Thank you, again!" she called, and waved back.

Chapter 13
1914

Helping Mary

As he promised, on the Friday, James set out at 6.00 am and cycled out to the farm to visit Mary and her children. He felt a sense of release as he mounted the brow of the hill that marked the edge of town and began to freewheel down the other side. It was as if a burden of responsibility lifted from his shoulders as he left the town behind him. He was going on pastoral business in one sense but at the same time it felt like taking a holiday. He enjoyed the fresh morning air, the vistas that opened up over the countryside, even the countryside smells. He was also looking forward to spending some time in Mary's company, knowing her to be a loyal friend, someone whom he could trust and someone who cared for him as well as needing to be cared for.

He joined Mary in the milking parlour and, this time, was able to be of more help. He pitched in with milking the cows and helped to muck out the milking parlour afterwards. Once these tasks were finished, Mary invited him back into the farmhouse for some breakfast, for which they were joined by the children.

"How are you all getting on, without Daddy here?" he asked.

Eleanor immediately burst into tears and buried her head in her mother's apron.

"It's really hard," Said Hannah. "We miss him terribly, but we are very proud of him and we are doing our best to help Mummy."
"They've been marvellous," agreed Mary. Hannah even cooked the dinner for us the other night, didn't you, precious?"

"And I washed up!" said David, "And I ate all my dinner up, even though it didn't taste as good as when Mummy cooks it!"

"That's good to hear," James said. "It will make it so much easier for Daddy to know that you are being a help to Mummy."

"I wish he would come back!" said Eleanor, her voice muffled as her face was still buried in Mary's lap.

"He will, as soon as he gets some leave, or when the war is over." James said, encouragingly.

"Why haven't you gone to the war?" asked David.

"Well I happen to think that fighting is wrong. Your Daddy thinks differently and I respect him for that, as he respects me. Someone has to stay at home to help and comfort all the soldiers' and sailors' families and that's what I think God wants me to do. Before Daddy went away, he asked me to keep an eye on you all and to make sure you are alright, so I'm going to do that as best as I can."

The meal over, the children went off to play, leaving Jacob alone with Mary. The conversation between them continued as they sat either side of the big oak table in the farmhouse kitchen.

"And you, how are you coping?" he asked her.

"I have to be brave, for the children, but it isn't easy. I've found a couple of old men from the nearby village who are glad of a few extra pennies and they are doing some bits and pieces around the farm. Janey Brown's in the same position as me, looking after the neighbouring farm while her husband's gone to fight. She has her Dad staying there too, but we've come to an arrangement to look after each other's children now and then to make things easier, like when we have to go to market.

"I hate to say this, but in some ways it's actually better not having Jacob here. We used to get so annoyed with each other and disagree about things so much. I'm free to be my own mistress now and to do things the way I want to do them. Does that sound awful?"

"No, I can understand", James agreed.

"But what about you, Pastor? What's the news of Win?"

"I'm going to her parent's house to see her and the boys over the weekend. I'll try to persuade her to come back, but I don't hold out much hope. She's pretty unhappy about the way I've been preaching against the war and the implications of that for her and the boys."

"Do you think, maybe she just wanted to be more consulted about things?"

"It could be, I did go ahead without warning her or talking about it very much. But it's not the first time there's been tensions between us. She's never found it easy being a Minister's wife."

"Well, I think she should feel herself blessed to have such a good man."

"You're too kind my dear! I think your Jacob should be very pleased to be married to you, as well."

"Well, there, we've got the compliments out of the way," said Mary. "Perhaps I should get on with my work."

"Is there anything more I can do while I'm here?" James asked, "I don't have to rush off anywhere."

"There's a broken gate up in one of the fields needs fixing if you're up to it. I can get young David to show you where and to fetch and carry for you while you be mendin' it."

"I'm willing to have a go, if you can provide me with the tools."

Mary found Jacob's tool box, called David and sent the two of them off. The main post of the gate had rotted through and one of the bars was split. David showed James where some timber was stored in one of the farm's outbuildings. James made a point of getting David to do whatever he was capable of doing. The young lad responded positively to being treated like a young man and they had the gate fixed by lunchtime.

"What do you think you'd like to do when you grow up?" James asked him, as they walked back to the farm.

"I'm not sure," he replied. "Dad would like me to run the farm but I thought of being a doctor or a minister, like you. I'd like to do something that will help people, not just make money. But being a doctor means dealing with blood and stuff and being a minister means having to stand up and talk in front of people. My teacher, Miss Jones, thinks I should be a politician. That's what she'd like to be but she can't because she's a woman. She told us she would be very happy if one of her pupils got to speak in parliament."

"Well all of those are very laudable careers, David. I wish you

well in the future whatever happens to you. There's no limit to what you can do if you are brave and put your mind to it."
James stayed for lunch with Mary and the children and then set off back to town.

"Would you like me to come back next Friday?" He said. "Friday's my official day off."

Mary's eyes glowed with appreciation,

"I don't want to impose on you Pastor," she said, but I'd like it, very much."

"I think we know each other well enough to drop the formalities, Mary," he said. "I'd be very happy if you would call me "James" from now on."

"I shall try to remember," she said. And with that, James mounted his bicycle and rode off down the drive.

Chapter 14
1914

A visit to Win

On the Friday evening, James caught the train to go and visit Win at her parents' home in Millborough, a town about 60 miles north of London. He'd arranged for a visiting preacher to stand in for him on the Sunday so that he could spend a whole weekend with the family. The boys were overjoyed to see him. He spent Saturday morning playing football with them in a big park nearby.

In the afternoon, he and Win went for a walk together. It was a beautiful, sunny afternoon. Everything was bathed in a golden, late summer sunshine. One of the most pleasant features of Millborough is its long, tree-lined promenades that stretch along the river banks either side of an imposing bridge. James and Win walked along the river in the shade of the chestnut trees that were just starting to change colour. The river was a hive of activity with people rowing up and down the river in hired boats.

Win suggested they sit on one of the benches in a shady spot. As they did so, James was about to start trying to persuade her to come back home and was trying to think of what to say. He had rehearsed it over and over in his mind in the train the previous night but now he couldn't think how to get started.

But before he could open up the conversation, Win started it for him and took it in an unexpected direction.

"James, I have something to ask you. I wonder if you would be so kind as to give your blessing to me going to the front to serve as a nurse? If I were a man, I would have enlisted. I believe some of my frustration with your pacifism is really my own frustration at being a woman and not being allowed to fight for my country. But if you won't go, why can't I? With my previous experience, the Queen Alexandra's Imperial Nursing Service would welcome me with open arms. I've asked Mummy and Papa and they are willing to look after the boys for us and to let you come and see them whenever you wish. I appreciate you couldn't do justice to your pastoral duties and look after the boys on your own. Papa's also willing to pay the fees for them to go to Millborough
High School."

James was taken aback.

"What can I say?' he mused. "I miss having the boys around but the chance to go to such a good school is an opportunity not to be missed. You would be doing good at the front. I would worry for you but I would also be immensely proud of you and my prayers would go with you all the way."

"And you can continue to do your work for God in Oakdale," Win continued. "I don't agree with your stand against the war, James, but I appreciate that it takes courage for you to take that stand. You may not be going to fight, but you are by no means a coward. And someone has to stay behind to comfort all those poor people whose sons and husbands are going to be killed."

James began to tell her about the visits he had made and the anguish and fear that so many of the women in the town were feeling, the absence of a man to do the lifting and maintenance jobs that their men would normally have done.

"It's not going to be long before men start to get injured and killed and someone needs to support the relatives and conduct the funerals. I'm the only Free Church minister left in the town now."

He told Win how, the day before, he had helped Mary at the farm and had promised to go and help once a week.

"That's very kind of you, James, Mary observed, "But do be careful. I don't think Jacob and Mary get on too well together and, if you are too nice to her while he's away, she might start to become inconveniently fond of you. However innocent the two of you are, there's a risk of people talking. Please don't forget me at the front. I do love you James and, when the war is over I promise to come home and try to be a dutiful wife."

He reached out and grasped her hand. Instead of pushing it away, she held it tightly.

Chapter 15
1936

Plans for the summer

In 1936 the month of May was dull and grey. Day after day thick clouds full of rain blew across the Atlantic and emptied their contents along the Welsh coast as the strong winds forced them into the mountains of Snowdonia.

For students, the summer term is always a time for intensive study with end of term exams looming large. Heulwen spent day after day either in her room or sitting in the college library reading over and over again her lecture notes and key passages in text books.

One afternoon, a couple of weeks into the summer term, she invited Awena round for tea and cakes, to give them both a bit of a break. The rain, once more, was lashing at the window.

"What an awful day!" Heulwen exclaimed.

"The rain just never seems to ease up," Awena agreed. "This time last year I spent most of my time sitting up on Roman Camp, doing my revision in the sunshine. The weather is so different this year. Changing the subject, though, have you discovered anything more about the mystery man—you know—your real father?"

"Not really, All I know is that Auntie B—my mother—was a teacher at a school in a place called Oakdale, in the North Midlands. She got to be head teacher when war broke out and all the men went off to the front. She told Mam that the man that got her pregnant was someone who was in the public eye and, when she knew she was pregnant, she left and came home to Wales to avoid a scandal—for him as much as for her.

"And then, among her belongings, we found a letter from someone called James which we think was probably from him. Reading between the lines of the letter it sounds as if he had done something with her that he was a ashamed of. I tell you what, I'll go and get it so you can have a look."

Heulwen jumped up from the edge of her bed and walked over to a chest of drawers and took out the letter for Awena to see.

Awena took it and read it through. She looked up and said, "Dear me! I wonder what they'd been up to?" A moment later she added,

"Had you thought of going to this Oakdale place to see if you can find any clues? If Your Auntie B was the head teacher of a school, there will be people still living there whom she taught and who will remember her. If this James man was part of her social circle, some of the people who remember her may be able to identify him. Gosh, he might still be living there. After all, it's only 23 years ago at the most."

"I had thought of doing that," Heulwen responded. "It would be a bit daunting, though, doing it on my own."

"Well, take a friend then!" Exclaimed Awena, "Take me—I'll come with you".

"Would you really?" Heulwen asked in amazement.

"It would be a nice little adventure for the summer vacation," Awena enthused. "I mean it, seriously. We could find a hotel or a guest house somewhere round there and do some walking at the same time. It's not far from the Peak District, which I've heard is quite beautiful—not unlike North Wales in some ways but without the sea. It'll be fun. Please say yes, I'd love to come father hunting with you."

" 'Father hunting'!" Heulwen exclaimed. "You make it sound like a safari! If we find him, I'm not planning to mount his head on the wall as a trophy!"

"I'm only joking! But you must admit it's exciting. Better than going to the seaside and sitting in a deck chair for a week! Go on, say yes; live dangerously!"

"Well, yes then. It's a deal. Thanks Awena, you're a real pal."

The next few weeks were taken up with revision and exams but, as soon as the last exam was finished, they spent two or three days visiting the local library and touring round bookshops to find out about guest houses and places of interest that they could visit on their trip.

Then they went their separate ways, Awena to her home in Carmarthen and Heulwen back to Hebron to spend a couple of weeks with Louise and Tom. They arranged to meet up at Chester station on the first Saturday of their holiday to travel on to Oakdale together.

Chapter 16
1914

The end of summer

August always brought a lull in the life of Oakdale chapel. Each year at the beginning of August the "stay works", as the local lingerie factory was known, would shut down for a week, enabling its workers to head off to Blackpool, Rhyl, Weston Super Mare or some other seaside resort. And for the rest of the month a fair proportion of the chapel congregation were busy helping local farmers with the harvest. This year there had been the additional disruption of the outbreak of war.

In contrast, September was always busy as church activities sprang into life once more and the weekly routine of midweek activities began again. Evenings became congested with meetings to plan this or prepare that. At the end of the month here was always a harvest festival weekend.

It was good to have made some sort of peace with Win. James felt that a load had lifted from his shoulders. It enabled him to work with more energy and enjoyment during the following week, preparing his sermons for Sunday and calling on further homes from the congregation where he knew a husband or father or son had gone to the war.

The September rush in 1914 began with a meeting of the deacons—those who were left. With Albert and Jacob and two other deacons away on military service, the usual committee of seven was down to four, Jim Naylor. the butcher, Frank Ryman, a retired pharmacist; Gwendoline Clewes, the owner of a local haberdashery business and Edith Keaton, a retired midwife.

James had circulated an agenda to them the previous week and scheduled the meeting for Monday 7th of September. As the first item he had put "Election to diaconate vacancies".

However, on the Tuesday before the deacons were due to meet, a new development threw the agenda into question. James had just finished eating his evening meal when the doorbell rang. He opened the door to find two members of the congregation on the doorstep. One was Felicity Kent, a housewife whose husband had gone, like most of the local men, to join the Sherwood Foresters. With her was Edward Ferris, who kept an ironmonger's shop in the High Street. Both had unsmiling, determined expressions on their faces. James invited them in, but they declined the invitation.

"We've just come to deliver a letter; we believe it expresses the feelings of many of the congregation," said Mrs Kent.

"Just take it and read it, please," added Edward Ferris, as James once more encouraged them to come in. "It is a request for an item to be included in the agenda for the next Church Members' Meeting."

They turned and left. James closed the door and opened the letter. His head began to spin as he read:

> "We, the undersigned, wish to propose a motion of no confidence in Rev James Wortley as the pastor of Union Chapel, in view of his unpatriotic stance over the war and the fact that he and his wife have separated.".

Like all Congregationalist and Baptist churches, Union Chapel was governed on somewhat democratic lines. The business of the chapel was regularly brought for consideration to a meeting of all the members. A decision by a majority of the members was binding on the deacons and the minister—a reflection of the conviction that God could speak to (and through) any member of the congregation.

James had no way of telling how many of the congregation the Kents and the Ferrises spoke for. It was a worrying development and, as Win was not there for him to talk it over with, it weighed heavily on his mind so that he slept badly that night. If Felicity and Edward represented a sufficient proportion of the congregation, or could persuade a sufficient number to their point of view, it would mean the end of James' time in Oakdale, the loss of his home as well as his employment and the need to search for a new position.

The next day he called in to see each of the members of the diaconate in turn to alert them of the new development. Three of them dismissed it as just a minority view which didn't represent the feelings of most of the congregation. "Don't worry Mr Wortley, it'll all blow over, you'll see," said Gwendoline Clewes, giving him an encouraging pat on the arm. But Jim Naylor told a different story,

"Appen I knows a few folk as feels the same way. I should think on't if I were you." he warned.

By the end of the afternoon James felt in need of some encouraging company.

He remembered that the Autumn term had begun at the local school that day so, at the end of the afternoon, he called in to see how Bethan had fared on her first day as head.

He knocked gently on the door of the head's office and heard her call "Come in".

"Oh, Reverend Wortley, How wonderful to see you, do come and take a seat," she exclaimed as he stood in the doorway.

James sat down in the armchair in the corner of the room. It seemed only a few days ago that he had sat in the same place facing Albert Whale. It was odd to see Bethan on the other side of the big desk.

"I thought I'd pop in to encourage you and to find out how your first day has gone." He explained."

"It's been a lovely day," she reported. Some of the children have been very sweet, one or two have told me that they are glad that I'm their head. The other staff have been very supportive. It's been quite difficult to fit in the teaching on top of everything else, though. I had to leave a class on their own for five minutes this afternoon because a child was taken ill in another class and I needed to help the teacher deal with the situation."

"I'm glad it's gone well." James said, "I'm sure you'll get more and more confident as the days go by. Don't hesitate to come to me for advice if you have any problems."

"Actually, Mr Wortley, I have quite a list of things I'd like to discuss with you. I wondered if we could meet together some time soon? I thought of inviting you round to my cottage for tea one day…"

James cut her short,

"Well, first of all, can I say that 'Mr Wortley' sounds rather formal since we are colleagues now. I give you permission to call me 'James'.

"Secondly, I'd be very pleased to have a meeting with you about your ideas for the school, but the next two weeks are very busy for me, I wonder if it could wait for a couple of weeks when things will be quieter?

"And then, though I really do appreciate your invitation to tea, I think we need to be careful not to give any misleading impressions, We are both important people in the community—in the public eye as it were—and, if it were known that I was coming to your cottage on my own, some people might draw the wrong conclusion and tongues might start to wag. It's probably best if we meet at the school. I'm not brushing you off, really, I'm just trying to protect you."

"Alright, I suppose that's wise," she agreed. And they made an appointment to meet together in her office at the school in three weeks time.

❋❋❋

Friday came round again and, true to his promise, James went out to the farm to visit Mary and help with the milking and any odd jobs that needed doing. He took the pony and trap this time and was there in time once more to help with the milking, before joining Mary in the farmhouse kitchen afterwards.

James was beginning to feel at home and insisted that Mary stayed seated at the table while he made them a cup of tea.

"It seems strange without the children here." He commented. "Did they get off to school alright?"

"Eleanor was s bit tearful" Mary reported. "It's only her second day and it's a long way for a five year old to walk into town. She've got the other two to look after her, though, I think she'll be alright."

There was a light of appreciation and affection in Mary's eyes as he put the mug down in front of her.

"It's so 'andsome to be waited on!" she said.

"Don't mention it," James said as he sat down opposite her. "You must be exhausted from all the work on the farm and looking after the children. Any news of Jacob yet?"

"I know he got to Plymouth safely and spent a week or so there before boarding ship. They can't tell you what ship they be on or where they be sailing to, in case the Germans gets to know. No news is good news, though. The Admiralty would tell me soon enough if anything bad happened to him."

"And what about Win?" Mary asked, after a pause. "Did you get to see her last weekend, I know you was a bit worried about it."

"We got on quite well, actually," he replied. "She was more understanding of my point of view than before. But she dropped a surprise on me; she's decided to go off and join the QAs,—you know, the army nurses. Her father has volunteered to fund the boys to go to a very good school in Millborough and Mary's happy for me to have them back here in the holidays sometimes."

"I'm glad she's more understanding. You'll miss her though, and the boys. It puts you in the same position as all of us ladies who are having to make do without our men around. You must have been finding it lonely without her and the boys at home."

I have," James agreed. It's especially hard when there are difficult things to face on my own."

James was thinking of the letter from Edward Ferris and Felicity Kent. Mary seemed to sense that there was a particular situation he had in mind, that something was troubling him.

"Is there something in particular that's on your mind at the moment? She asked.

"Aye, there is " he said.

"Is it something I can help with?" she probed, "They say a burden shared is a burden halved. I can keep a confidence."

"Well, you'll know, soon enough," James mused, "A couple of people have asked for there to be a vote of no confidence me as pastor—to get me to leave."

A look of shock and pain passed over Mary's face.

"But that's awful!" she sympathised. "Why ever would they want to do that?"

"They are saying that I'm unpatriotic and it dishonours the lads who are out there fighting—and it brings the church into disrepute in the town. They've also noticed that Win hasn't been around and they are concluding that our marriage is not as it should be."

"Oh, James," Mary exclaimed, "You poor thing; that's so worrying." Her hand reached out and briefly touched his arm. "I'm sure that there won't be many people in the congregation who agree with them. It will all blow over, you'll see."

"Thank you Mary. I know I have a loyal friend in you. I appreciate being able to share it with you. Please pray for me."
"James looked up and their eyes met.

I will, Pastor —James —I will," she said, fervently."

❋❋❋

On Sunday morning, James preached a sermon based on Isaiah 2

> "And it shall come to pass in the last days
> that the mountain of the Lord's house shall be established as
> the top of the mountains
> and shall be exalted above the hills
> and all nations shall flow unto it
> And many people shall go and say,
> 'Come ye and let us go up to the house of the Lord,
> the house of the God of Jacob
> and he will teach us his ways…
> and he shall judge among the nations
> and shall rebuke many people
> and they shall beat their swords into plowshares
> and their spears into pruning hooks
> nation shall not lift up sword against nation
> neither shall they study war any more.' "

"How God's heart must break at the carnage and the conflict between nations that is taking place?" he began. "Surely his judgement must be ready to fall on the nations that are involved."

"But God promises a greater time to come, when the nations flow together instead of setting themselves against one another, a time when instruments of aggression will be transformed into instruments of production, when nations will seek to feed each other rather than to kill one another. Let the promise of that glorious time to come comfort us and strengthen us as we go through the turmoil and anguish of these terrible days."

***

The next day, on the Monday evening, James met with the deacons. They decided to call a member's meeting on 12th October with four items on the agenda:

- Motion proposing a vote of no confidence in Rev James Wortley as Pastor.
- Election of deacons.
- Appointment of new Church Secretary
- Appointment of new Church Treasurer.

***

Although James had booked the meeting with Bethan at the school for three weeks time, it seemed to come round very quickly.

As she had hinted, Bethan had a long list of suggestions for improving the school and its operation. Unfortunately, almost all involved expenditure at a time when funds were stretched to the limit and James found himself again and again giving the same response.

"All these suggestions are good, Bethan," he said in as encouraging voice as he could manage, "But there just aren't the funds available to put them into effect."

There were, fortunately, some suggestions that he was able to endorse more positively. There was a patch of waste ground at the back of the chapel buildings. Bethan could see it being turned into a garden where children could be taught horticultural skills while producing vegetables which could be sold to the local greengrocer, thus increasing the local food supply and earning money for the school funds. "We could build a chicken run and produce eggs, as well." James suggested.

A more controversial suggestion from Bethan was the introduction of citizenship lessons. It was evident from the way she described the idea that she intended to promote socialist ideals and to prepare the girls for a future where they could take a full part in the political life of the nation.

"I have some sympathy with what you want to achieve," he said, reassuringly, "but there will be many people in the community who would oppose what you are trying to do, especially where preparing young women to have the vote is concerned. As you know, I've already attracted some negative reactions from the local population and I'm anxious not to add fuel to the fire, at least, not at this moment."

"I understand," Bethan, replied, "I think this move to have you ousted from your job is appalling. You have my support, and my prayers. Thinking about the church meeting, I was wondering whether I could volunteer to take on the Church Secretary role? Since I've stepped into Albert Whale's shoes in one job I thought it might make sense if I did it in the other as well."

"Well, find yourself a proposer and seconder and we'll put you to the vote along with any other candidates." James told her.

Chapter 17
1914

Harvest

O ver in France, even as Bethan and James were talking, the British Expeditionary Force was facing a crucial turning point. The German armies were entrenched in an unassailable position in the hills to the East of the River Aisne. To attack them, the allied forces had to cross a river and then advance 500 yards uphill, into the teeth of machine gun and artillery fire. It was the beginning of a long stalemate, the start of warfare on an industrial scale, and of life in the trenches.

In Oakdale, the staff at the local post office suddenly faced an influx of letters encased in the standard armed services brown envelope, all bearing bad news.

James made his usual Friday visit to Sandybrook Farm to help with the milking and to do any other odd jobs he could do to make Mary's life more easy. During the week a couple of soldiers had come to requisition his pony for military service, so James cycled to the farm. He ended up staying for some lunch and was riding back into Oakdale about 2pm. As he reached the summit of the uphill slope that led back into the town, he passed a young telegraph boy who had been pushing his bike up the other side of the hill and had stopped at the summit to remount. He recognised him as one of the lads from the Chapel Boys' Brigade company.

"Hello. Graham," he called, "How's it going?"

"A - do, Reverend," The boy replied, "I'm fair rooshed off me feet today. One of the regiments that has a lot of Oakdale lads in it 'as sooffered soome terrible losses. I've been 'ere there and everywhere delivering envelopes, all of them bad news. The post mistress wanted them to go out straight away. Poor Mrs Appleby's lost her 'oosband and two of 'er sons."

"Dear me, how awful," James replied. "But don't let me keep you from your work. Take care." Instead of going home, James went straight to Mrs. Appleby's house. Sarah Appleby lived in a cottage on the Stoke Road,. Her husband and her three grown up sons had all enlisted and gone off leaving her on her own.

Sarah herself answered the door. Without saying a word she collapsed into his arms and buried her face in his shoulder, sobbing. The sobs continued for what seemed like an age.

"Come and sit down, my dear." He said, gently, leading her into the parlour. She was still incapable of speaking and hardly managing to stand. She pointed to the opened brown envelope and the letter lying on the table. He picked it up and read it.

"I saw Graham Ashworth on the Sheffield Road," He said. He told me he'd delivered the message to you. I came straight away." Sarah nodded. She still couldn't speak—not with words. Her eyes spoke volumes, full of the horror and shock of her triple bereavement.

There was nothing he could say that was of any sense or any comfort. He sat with her in silence for another ten minutes or so. Then he laid his hand gently on her wrist and prayed. He prayed for comfort for her, for strength to carry on. Then he recited the 23rd Psalm,

"Though I walk through the valley of the shadow of death. I will fear no evil for thou art with me…"

The sobs started again, more gently this time – a trickle of grief instead of a flood.

"Let me get you a cup of tea," he suggested, lamely. There was a kettle already simmering on the range. He searched around and found a teapot and a cup, some sugar and milk in the pantry.

"Thank you Pastor," she said quietly, as he put the cup into her hand.

"Is there a neighbour I can call to come and be with you for a while?" he asked.

"Mrs Miller next door is a good friend." She said.

James went next door and knocked.

A middle aged woman answered the door. "Mrs Miller?" he asked. He reported Sarah's bereavement to her. "I wondered if you could come and keep her company for a while?"

"I will indeed, she agreed." He went back to Sarah's house with her and took his leave. "I'll be back later on to see how you are," he promised."

✳✳✳

Through the weekend and throughout the next week, day after day, James received news of one Oakdale man after another who had been killed or wounded on the battlefield. As the minister, his responsibility was to call at each home where there had been a bereavement, to offer comfort, practical help where it was needed and to start to make plans for the funeral. He struggled to keep up with the tide of deaths, spending almost all of every day the next week visiting homes where loved ones had been killed. The grief of the families was made even harder to bear by the necessity for their bodies to be interred in France. With such a heavy toll of fatalities and all military and transport resources engaged in supplying the war effort, there was no possibility of bringing the bodies of the dead soldiers home. For the families, that made it impossible to carry out the normal rituals of mourning. Without a body, there was no funeral, no graveside farewell. The best that could be managed was a memorial service in a church or chapel. Such services were to become part of the daily routine for James in the ensuing weeks, along with the constant visits to comfort the wives, mothers, children, and sweethearts of those who had fallen.

He and the deacons decided to cancel the chapel's annual harvest supper. It didn't seem appropriate to have a time of jollity and fun when so many of the congregation were grieving. The normal harvest thanksgiving services took place, though, on the last Sunday in September, with the chapel decorated as usual and filled with the rich aroma of the fruit and flowers.
The morning service began with a traditional hymn, "Come ye thankful people come." In the third verse, James realised that the writer was seeing mankind as a harvest:

> "For the Lord our God shall come
> And shall take his harvest home…"

His eyes started to fill with tears and his voice choked as he thought of the terrible reaping that was taking place—young men and boys being mown down and killed in their thousands. He could find comfort in the thought of them being gathered into God's presence and yet he struggled with the awfulness of it. In his sermon he tried to bring comfort by holding out the hope of Heaven for those who love God and by honouring the courage of those who had given their lives. He reminded the congregation of the brevity of life, that death can come suddenly in many ways, not only through war, and he urged the necessity for everyone to be prepared to face their maker and to live life with eternity in view.

After the service, people were in no hurry to go. Little groups stood around talking, both inside the chapel and in the street outside. There was a stunned, subdued atmosphere. Tears were being shed, comfort given.

Even Bethan was subdued as she greeted James at the end of the service. "It's such a sad day, James," she observed. "You feel it too, don't you? All these men cut down in their prime. It's so awful." She took his hand and pressed it warmly between hers, holding it a little longer than usual.

The evening service ended with an evening hymn, "Sun of my soul thou saviour dear." One of the verses included the words,

> "Be every mourner's sleep tonight,
> Like infant's slumbers, pure and light."

"Lord," James prayed quietly as the congregation were singing that verse, "Lord, Please comfort all those who have lost loved ones. And please keep Win safe and be with her, wherever she is."

Chapter 18
1914

Falling Leaves

J ames received a letter from Win on the Monday morning. It included news of the boys and ended, "I have been accepted into the QAs and will be on my way soon to a hospital in France. Thank you for allowing me to go. I hope I shall be able to do some good there. Please forgive me for my anger which came largely out of concern for our boys. I understand why you opposed the war and I am proud of your courage. I will pray for you as you seek to help and comfort those who are facing grief and concern for their loved ones. Please pray for me that I may be kept safe and be able to be a help and comfort to the men who are wounded. I love you, your Win."

✳✳✳

"Good evening everyone, can we come to order, please?"

James tried hard to project his voice above the hubbub of voices. The turn out at the church members' meeting was larger than usual, even though so many of the men were away fighting in the war.

The babble of voices gradually subsided.

"Thank you," he continued, "In view of the content of the agenda this evening I am not going to take the chair as usual. Miss Clewes has volunteered to take that responsibility and the deacons and I propose that she be invited to take the chair in my place. Does anyone have any objection to raise?"

There was a silence, broken by the arrival of a handful of late arrivals who slipped in at the back of the hall.

"Those in favour of Miss Clewes taking the chair, please show," James added. A forest of hands shot up. "I think that's unanimous, be said. "Over to you, Miss Clewes."

"Thank you, Mr Wortley," Gwendoline said, "I'd like to start with a Bible reading and prayer. Then we shall have the election of deacons before we attend to the proposal that has come from Mrs. Kent and Mr. Ferris. When we get to that point I propose to give Rev Wortley the opportunity to say anything he wishes to say on the matter and for members of the church to question him further if they so desire. Then Rev Wortley will absent himself while we continue the discussion and come to a vote on it."

The gathered church members sat in attentive silence. Bethan Jones had succeeded in finding people to propose and second her for the vacancy for church secretary. There were no other applicants and so she was appointed, with only a handful of people voting against. Frederick Barker, a retired postman, was appointed to fill the other vacancy on the diaconate.

Eventually, Gwendoline gave James the opportunity to respond to the letter.

"I've only been here just over a year," he began, "but I've grown to love Oakdale and its people. I would love to continue serving you, but I'm in God's hands. The accusation has been brought against me that I am unpatriotic, because I have opposed the war. I would assert that one can love one's country and yet not agree with all that is done in its name. If criticising your country's behaviour is unpatriotic, then all the prophets in the Old Testament are as guilty as I am. I love my country and am proud to be British. But I believe our leaders have made a mistake in going to war. Europe has become like a school playground where two boys have started an unnecessary fight and all the others, including the prefects, have taken sides and joined in. The "big boys"—countries like ours and France and Germany—should have stopped the little boys—banged their heads together and told hem not to be so silly. I believe they should have refused to be sucked into the conflict. War and fighting only result in bloodshed and grief and the loss of precious young lives. In the end the time will come when the leaders of the nations that are at present at war will have to get around a table and find a way of negotiating a peace. Why not do it sooner, rather than later? This is a democratic country and we all as citizens have the opportunity to say, 'We will not have this.' Our men can choose to say 'I will not join in'.

"Having said that, in no way do I want to denigrate the sacrifices being made by our gallant lads on the front. I honour their bravery and courage as much as I bemoan their loss.

"As for the accusation about my relationship with Win, my dear wife, I will be honest and say that we did not see eye to eye over the war. Because of the stance I took we experienced some angry reactions from some local people—we even had a brick thrown through our window. Win feared for the safety of our two boys and was concerned that they might be bullied at school because of my stand. That was why she decided to take them home to live with their grandparents for the time being. I went to see her recently and our conversation was amicable. We understand and honour each other's point of view. We can disagree and still be friends—would that more of the human race were able to do the same. Win has recently decided to enlist as an army nurse and is already on her way to the front. We have put the boys into a good school in Millborough and they will be staying with their grandparents for the duration of the war.

"I don't think there is any more I need to say." James hesitated and looked around. Does anyone wish to ask any questions?

There was a silence. James turned to face Gwendoline.

"Thank you, pastor" she said. "I will be in touch just as soon as the meeting is over to let you know the result."

James took his leave and stepped out into the blustery dampness of the night. He walked home and made himself some cocoa. He felt on edge.

Back at the church hall one member after another spoke in favour of James. Mrs Allsop told how he had fixed her toilet, Mary reported how he had promised to Jacob to take care of her and her family and how he was trying to be faithful in carrying it out. Mrs Ryman spoke of her grief and how he had been a comfort to her. "I've sacrificed a husband and two sons in this war," she said. "I understand why Rev Wortley stood against it. If my boys had listened to him they might still be here."

Mrs Kent and Mr Ferris tried to argue their case but no-one else joined them. Eventually, Miss Clewes called for a vote. It was overwhelmingly against the proposal.

Gwendoline and Bethan called at the manse afterwards. James ushered them into his study.

"We are very pleased to report that the motion was defeated and the vast majority of the members want you to stay," reported Gwendoline. Bethan smiled, "I do hope you will," she added."

James did indeed stay and continued his work at Union Chapel. The Oakdale citizens had been shaken by the heavy casualties among the men who had gone to war in the local regiment. The jingoism and optimism that had been around during August and September evaporated and a cloud of anxiety and tension seemed to hover over the town. There was a further spate of casualties in October when some of the local battalions were involved in the fighting at Ypres. James continued his work, maintaining the weekly routine of worship, preaching at the Sunday services and providing emotional and practical support wherever he could to the families of the men who had died or been severely injured.

His weekly visit to Sandybrook Farm on Fridays became something of an oasis in his week, an escape from the responsibilities of running the church, and the opportunity to relax and be himself. It was refreshing to be outside and doing manual tasks instead of writing and talking all the time. He and Mary became increasingly secure in each other's friendship and confided in each other more and more.

Bethan's appointment as church secretary inevitably meant that she and James had reason to spend even more time in each other's company. As well as discussions about the running of the school, there was now church business to discuss—the notices to be given out at the Sunday services and agendas and minutes for deacons' and church members' meetings. James tried to make sure that conversations with her took place at the school but she became aware of his Friday visits to Sandybrook Farm.

"James, do you mind if I challenge you about something?" she asked one day. "You refused to come to tea with me because you didn't want tongues to wag but I find that you are regularly visiting Mary Hollinshead and having meals with her at Sandybrook Farm. Do you think that tongues are more likely to wag about you and me than about you and her? If so, I'd like to know why. Do you think I am less to be trusted? If so. I'm rather hurt."

James flushed and hesitated. He could see clearly the injustice she had pointed out. The fact was that he probably did see her as more of a threat than Mary. Although he had become fond of Mary, he trusted her not to act in any improper way and guessed that other people would too. In addition, the farm was well out of town, whereas Bethan's cottage was almost in the High Street. Part of his insecurity with Bethan came from her feisty and slightly flirtatious attitude, her refusal to accept things as they are, her willingness to push boundaries. Part of his insecurity, he realised, also sprang from his own body's reaction to hers—her hourglass figure, her flawless complexion and the way she moved. It wasn't so much that he didn't trust her, as that he didn't trust himself.

"I understand what you are saying," he replied. "I have been inconsistent and you are right to be hurt. I am so sorry."

"So, next Thursday, instead of us meeting at school, will you come and have tea with me at my cottage? If you say yes, I'll forgive you."

"Yes, I will" he responded, "Then you're forgiven," she said. "Shake on it?" She held out her hand. He took it, intending to shake it, then realised she was raising her hand towards his lips. He brushed his lips lightly across her fingers. She looked at him with a slightly mischievous gleam in her eye.

✳✳✳

When the next Thursday came he and Bethan spent a pleasant couple of hours together. It was a cold November day and there was a fire in the grate. Bethan had baked a delicious lemon cake specially for the occasion. She maintained a professional distance from him, physically and in the way she spoke. They discussed plans for the school nativity play and the fact that the local authority had given exemption from education to some of the older boys because their services were needed on family farms. James reported on a meeting he had had with a high ranking army officer who was looking for premises to commandeer for a hospital to house men who had come back severely wounded from the front.

"I think I managed to convince him that the church rooms and the school room would not be suitable," James said. "He was concerned that access for ambulances would be difficult. He was going to look at the Grammar School afterwards."

As James took his leave, Bethan shook hands with a firm and professional handshake.

✳✳✳

When James arrived at Sandybrook Farm on the last Friday in October, he was immediately aware of a change in Mary. She was smiling and happy. "Guess what!" she said as soon as she saw him. "I've had a postcard from Jacob!" She handed it to James, "You can read it!" she said. The card was postmarked from Valparaiso, in Chile. Apparently, Jacob's ship was in the South Pacific with a small fleet of other vessels. The weather was good, they had had some time ashore. He sounded in good spirits and sent his love to her and the children.

"I'm so glad he's safe!" James exclaimed. You must
be delighted."

He kept to himself the thought that James must have rounded
Cape Horn with its notoriously rough seas.

The following Wednesday afternoon, however, James responded
to the ringing of the doorbell at the manse and was surprised to
find Mary standing on the doorstep. "Can I come in?" she asked.
"Of course," James replied.

As soon as he had ushered her into his study, Mary took out of her
purse a brown envelope. James' heart sank as he saw it. He had
seen too many others like it in the last two months. Unable to
speak without crying, she handed it to him and he read the words.

"Regret to inform you Chief Petty Officer Jacob Hollinshead
reported missing in action, believed killed…"

"Oh, my dear!" James exclaimed and knelt beside the chair,
putting his arm round her shoulder to comfort her.

"It's the worst kind of news, isn't it?" he commented, after a
while. "It's distressing, because you know something is wrong
and yet it offers hope, because it doesn't say he is definitely
killed. If it were more final you could come to terms with it and
move on. Instead, it leaves you in limbo."

"A thousand thoughts have gone through my head since I got it,
she said." I've had him sinking to the bottom of the sea, taken
prisoner, clinging to wreckage in the water. If only I knew what
had happened!"

James gently laid his hand on her arm and prayed a prayer for
strength for her and for God to protect Jacob and bring him home,
if he were still alive.

"What am I going to tell the children?" she asked, when James had finished his prayer.

"I think the best thing for their sake might be to say nothing," James suggested. "At least until you know more. You don't want them to be worried without any need. I know that would be hard for you, though, to carry on as if nothing had happened. If you can't hide your feelings, then it might be best to tell them and share it with them. If you decide not to tell them you will need to be careful who else you *do* tell. It would be very unpleasant for them to hear it from someone else."

The next day, James read the account of the Battle of Coronel in the paper and realised that Jacob's ship would have been involved. The newspaper described a terrible defeat for the British fleet commanded by Admiral Sir Christopher Craddock and the sinking of several ships. Almost certainly Jacob had been on one of the vessels that had been sunk.

James went out to Sandybrook Farm at once to make sure that Mary was aware. Jacob proposed that Mary should tell the children, after all, since they knew their father was in that part of the world and there was a strong possibility that they might overhear news of the battle from someone else. James took the pony and trap from the farm back into town to meet the children from school and volunteered to explain the situation to them for Mary as he brought them home.

"You must be strong for Mummy," he said before he took his leave of them in the evening. "We don't know what has happened to Daddy. We know that the ship he was on was sunk and many of the sailors lost their lives but for all we know he could have escaped. There's a slim chance that he may have done. Let's pray that he did and hope for the best."

"Thank you, Reverend Wortley," said David, politely. "I'll do my best to look after Mummy."

"Good lad," he replied.

❄❄❄

On and off throughout the following week James kept wondering how Mary and the children were coping. When he arrived at the farm on the Friday, his first thought was to ask her if she had heard any more news of Jacob and how they were bearing the strain of not knowing what had happened to him. However, before he could say a word, Mary greeted him with some excitement, saying,

"I've got something exciting for you to do today. Are you any good at ploughing?"

James had to confess that this was an area in which he had no expertise at all. But Mary was not deterred.

I'm planning to put the big top field to growing some wheat. It's only got a slight slope and it faces south, so it ought to produce a reasonable crop and the price of wheat is rising. At best I'll produce some grain that we can use ourselves. If I'm lucky I might have some to sell. Anyhow, we need to plough the field to start with. I've borrowed a plough and a pair of horses from my friend Jenny. I'm counting on you to come and help me!"

As soon as the milking was done and they'd had a cup of tea, Mary took James to the stable where the horses were tethered. "I'll deal with the horses," she said. All I need you to do is to sit on the plough and make sure we go straight. The best thing is to keep your eyes on a fixed point and head for it. Thank the Lord he's given us some nice weather for it."

The weather was indeed dry and sunny for the time of year. Mary tramped ahead of them, holding the horses' heads and encouraging them with praise and gentle pats on the nose, while James sat on the plough and tried to keep it steady. He was amazed at how Mary was able to assert her authority over the huge carthorses and how eagerly they worked under her encouragement. The job was done by lunchtime. Only then did James broach the subject of Jacob.

"I had a letter from an Admiral," Mary said, "He said Jacob were on the *HMS Good Hope* which were sunk in the battle. Without the body they can't say for sure that he died but they think it were likely."

"What do you think, yourself?" James asked, gently.

"I don't know," she replied. "Logically, I can't see that he could be alive. The Admiral doesn't seem to think he could be. But there's something inside me that makes me feel he isn't dead." We'll just have to wait and see, I suppose."

Chapter 18
1936

A Summer's Adventure

H i, Awena!" Heulwen jumped up and down and waved as
she spotted her friend's sandy coloured, bobbed hair
among the crowd coming along the platform.

Awena quickened her pace as much as the large suitcase she was
carrying would allow her.

"How's your journey been, so far?" Heulwen asked as they met.

"Not too bad," Awena replied. "It's been a long trip, though."

"We've still got a way to go, I'm afraid. Down to Crewe first,
then we change again to get onto the line to Oakdale. That will be
a stopping train that calls at every village and hamlet on the way.
We've just got time to get something to eat in the
refreshment rooms."

"Oh, good, I'm starving!" Awena replied.

The rest of the journey went without a hitch. They arrived at
Oakdale in bright sunshine at five o' clock in the afternoon.

"How far is it to Belle Vue Road?" Awena asked the lady ticket collector as they walked through the barrier.

"It's only a short step, ma'am" she reassured her, "but it's uphill I'm afraid. Turn left outside the station, cross the High Street and you'll find a flight of steps. Belle Vue's at the top. If it's the guest house you're wanting, turn left."

They thanked her, followed the directions and, somewhat flushed and perspiring from the exertion of carrying their luggage up the hill, they arrived about a quarter of an hour later at the Belle Vue Guest House, where they had booked a room for the week. The room was pleasantly comfortable with twin beds and a view across the town to fields on the hills in the distance beyond. They had a table to themselves in the dining room when they reported for the evening meal. A genial, middle-aged couple occupied another table. Four young people, two men and two ladies, sat at another—they had the appearance of being walkers or cyclists— fit and healthy. A man sat in a corner on his own—probably a commercial traveller, they decided, as he seemed to be on familiar terms with the landlady.

"So, here we are in Oakdale!" Awena exclaimed as they ate their evening meal, "Ready to start the 'father hunt'."

"It's exciting," agreed Heulwen. "I feel quite nervous. But where do I begin?"

"Well, tomorrow's Sunday," Awena mused, "I suggest we go to church. There's bound to be someone there who can point us in the right direction—and even if there isn't, we can pray for guidance. Guest houses often have details of local church services. Let's ask the landlady."

The landlady directed them to a notice board on the landing outside the dining room. Headed "Places of Worship", it included a bewildering array. In addition to St Aelfred's parish church there was a Roman Catholic church, the Salvation Army, A Methodist chapel, a Foursquare Gospel mission, and the Union Chapel.

"Which one shall we go to?" Awena asked,
"Well, replied Heulwen. I can't imagine Auntie B going to the Roman Catholic Church or the Church of England. She was definitely chapel—we all are. I never saw her in a Salvation Army uniform and the Foursquare Gospellers have only been going for a few years, so I reckon it's the Methodists or Union Chapel. Look, under 'Union Chapel' it says it says 'Baptist and Congregational'. Our village chapel back home is Congregational so I reckon that's where Auntie B would have felt at home. Let's go there."

On the Sunday morning, after a hearty breakfast, they set off to have a look around the little town and to find the chapel in time for the service. Finding the chapel was easy. They retraced their way down the flight of steps towards the town, turned left along the High Street and there it was, an enormous building on the other side of the road. Beyond an imposing gateway one flight of steps led up to a big main door. On either side, two other sets of steps led downwards from the gateway to a basement. Awena drew Heulwen's attention to a smaller noticeboard alongside the one that advertised the chapel services. It said "Free Church Elementary School", with an arrow pointing down the steps to the basement.

"A chapel with a school—I think we might be on the right track," she said.

The service was not due to begin for another hour and a half, so they walked along the High Street, identified some eating places where they might go for a meal later and found a pleasant park where they sat in the sunshine for a while before walking back to the chapel for the service.

The congregation was a fair size—between two and three hundred people—but the chapel was evidently built for twice that number. A gallery ran all the way around three sides and huge, tall windows, lightly stained, shed a yellowish light on the congregation. At the front the pipes of a substantial organ were decorated in red and gold. Below the organ loft was a high pulpit and in front of that a communion table. The regular minister was away on holiday, so a visiting preacher led the service.

As the strains of the last hymn died away and the preacher pronounced the blessing, Awena and Heulwen hesitated, not wanting to rush out too quickly, hoping that someone would come and speak to them and maybe offer some information that would help them with their quest.

A young man who appeared to be in his late twenties spotted them and walked across the chapel to greet them. He was tall, slim but broad shouldered with curly, dark hair and a sun bronzed face out of which twinkled a pair of very blue eyes.

"Hello, I don't think I've seen you here before," he said, holding out a hand. "Are you new to the town?"

Heulwen and Awena both reached out simultaneously to take his hand with the embarrassing result that he ended up taking two of Awena's fingers and three of Heulwen's at the same time and shaking both their hands together. Heulwen thought to herself, "Oh dear we're looking too eager!"

"We're here on holiday…" Awena began but Heulwen interrupted. "I'm following the trail of an aunt of mine," she said. "She used to be a teacher in Oakdale, at the beginning of the Great War. We thought it would be interesting to follow in her footsteps."

She thought she had best be cautious in the way she introduced her mother in case she gave away secrets that might be damaging to anyone still alive in the town.

The young man suddenly looked even more interested, "What was her name?" He asked.

"Bethan Jones," Heulwen replied.

"Miss Jones?" The man's eyes lit up. "She was my favourite teacher. When I was seven or eight I was in love with her. I worshipped the ground she walked on. She was so beautiful. And kind. She always had time to listen to you. And she used to make lessons fun. She had a wonderful sense of humour. So she was your Aunt? Well I never! Yes, now you mention it, I think I can see a likeness."

"How amazing that you remember her!" Heulwen exclaimed. "I see you have a school in the church basement. Is that where she used to teach?"

"Yes," responded the young man. "I can show you around if you like. Hang on, the caretaker is over there, I'll go and get the keys from him. He quickly dived across the chapel to catch a man on the other side who was one of a huddle of people in conversation.

Heulwen and Awena looked at each other.

"He's gorgeous!" Awena mouthed, silently. "Hands off, he's mine!" Heulwen mouthed back. Awena wrinkled her nose and shook her head in a gesture of mock aggression and Heulwen momentarily stuck her tongue out. They quickly regained their composure as the young man came back.

"I'm sorry, I haven't introduced myself," he said. " My name's

David – David Hollinshead. And you are?"

"I'm Awena and this is Heulwen."

"Those are unusual names," he commented. "Are you Welsh by any chance?"

" 'Awena' means 'Muse' and 'Heulwen' means 'Sunshine'," Heulwen explaimed. "We are both training to be teachers at a college in North Wales. So this is definitely the chapel that my Aunt attended and she taught in the school downstairs?"

"Looks like it," David said. "Come, let me show you round."

They went out of the front of the chapel, down the stairs to the basement where David unlocked a big, main door and let them into the schoolrooms.

There were four classrooms, separated by movable wooden partitions, each of which had windows above chest height. The school hall doubled as a church hall at evenings and weekends. There were two separate playgrounds, one for boys and another for girls and infants. They passed a door that had a sign saying "head teacher's office." "Only the head has the key to the office, he explained, otherwise I'd let you in there as well."

Heulwen thought her heart would burst at the frustration of not being able to enter the room that must have been her mother's "inner sanctum".

"Thank you so much for showing us round, you've been most kind, she said."

"Don't worry, I've enjoyed it," he replied, then asked, "How long are you staying in in Oakdale?"

"Just for the week," Heulwen replied. "We plan to see some of the local scenery, perhaps to do some walking. Are there any local beauty spots you'd like to recommend?"

"I don't know about beauty spots," he responded, "but one place I would recommend you visit is Sandybrook Farm, it's about a mile out of town. I think it's a very special place, but I'm biased because I'm the farmer. I was wondering if I could invite you to come for afternoon tea one day. Would Tuesday be convenient?"

"That would be lovely!" the two girls said, almost in unison.

That's great! I'll come and pick you up about 2pm. Where are you staying?"

"The Belle Vue Guest House," said Heulwen, "Do you know it?"

"I do indeed. Tuesday it is, then."

Chapter 19
1914

Christmas

"Once in royal David's City
Stood a lowly cattle shed
Where a mother laid her baby
In a manger for his bed."

David Hollinshead's clear treble voice echoed round the chapel. The nervous expression that clouded his face at the start of the carol changed to a broad grin of relief and pride as he reached the end of the verse. Then the congregation joined in—those who were able; a number of them found that their eyes had filled with tears as they heard the first verse of the familiar carol sung so beautifully and they were still fighting back the tears as the second verse began.

It was the start of the school carol service and nativity play, held in the chapel on the next to last day of the term, with a congregation of parents, teachers and friends of the school. There were more carols, some Bible readings, all done by children, and a nativity play, in which David's sister, Hannah, played the part of Mary and young Eleanor had her own moment of glory as she appeared among the angels.

Refreshments were served in the hall afterwards and James tried to spread himself among the parents, giving each one a personal greeting. He spotted Mary and the three children who were in conversation with another family and made a point of going over to them and giving each of the children praise for the parts they had played. "You must be so proud of them!" he said to Mary. Bethan, as head teacher, was also trying to circulate and speak to everyone, as James was doing. She walked past James and Mary and the children and, as she did so, ruffled David's hair, "My little star!" she said, "You sang like an angel!" David flushed with pride. Then she looked at James and said, "Can I see you for a moment before you go? I've got something for you."

James continued talking to Mary and the children for a few moments. "I'll see you tomorrow morning," he said to Mary, as they left. Then he continued to circulate among the parents and staff and helped to put the chairs away in the hall. Eventually everyone had gone except Bethan, himself and the caretaker. Bethan dismissed the caretaker, "Thanks for all you've done, you've been brilliant. You get home, I'll lock up. Have a happy Christmas!"

She turned to James. "Can you just step into the staff room for a moment," she asked.

In the staff room, she picked up a small package and placed it in his hands.

"I'm off back to Wales for Christmas in the morning, so I won't see you until after the new year. I just want to say thank you for all your support and encouragement," Bethan explained. "It's meant so much. I've bought you a little Christmas present. I hope you like it."

"Thank you, that's kind of you," he said. "May I open it now?"

"Yes, please do, she replied."

It was a copy of *The Mystery of the Kingdom of God*, by Albert Schweitzer.

"I was intending to buy that myself! It's only just been published!" David exclaimed, "Thank you so much—but I haven't got anything for you!"

"Don't worry," Bethan said. "There's something you can give me right now that will make me very happy." She gestured with her eyes above James' head and he looked up to realise that, unwittingly, he was standing under a sprig of mistletoe.

Before he had time to react, Bethan had raised her lips and made contact with his. James didn't turn his face, but took her by the shoulders and gently indicated a desire for her to move away.

"Please, don't push me away," she murmured. "What harm is there in a Christmas kiss under the mistletoe, just once a year? Relax. Just hold me and let it happen."

"She reached out, put her arms round the back of his neck and pulled him to her again. Her lips were soft and yielding. He put his arms around her. She slid her arms down until they were round his waist and held her body close to his. They stayed there for what must have been a minute but seemed like ten."

"Thank you," she said in a husky voice. "You can go now. Dear James, have a happy Christmas."

"Bethan, I…"

"No, don't say a word. Don't spoil it," she said, firmly. "Go!"

James picked up his present, turned and went, his mind and emotions in a turmoil. He felt excited, duped, valued, loved, used, ashamed all at the same time. Bethan had broken down his defences—changed the dynamics of their relationship inappropriately and inextricably. Where would things go from there? Or was he reading too much into a bit of seasonal fun?

✳✳✳

James cycled out to Sandybrook Farm the next morning, as usual arriving early enough to help with the milking. He had taken with him a large tin of biscuits and a Christmas pudding as a Christmas present for Mary and the children. He handed them over to Mary when they returned to the kitchen after cleaning out the milking parlour.

"I hope you all have a pleasant Christmas," he said. "I know it's going to be difficult for you without Jacob here. In one way I wish I could be with you myself but I can't be in two places at once and I really want to spend some time with Matthew and Edward. I'm travelling down there on Monday and then I'll stay until after Christmas.

"I shall miss you, James," said Mary. Her eyes started to fill with tears which she blinked back. "You don't know how secure it makes me feel just to know that you are there in the manse and I can call on you whenever I need you. I shall be on edge and sad until you get back. You've been such a tower of strength these last months. I can't thank you enough for all you've done. I don't know what I would have done without you. I've got a Christmas present for you, too. I haven't had time to wrap it because I was still finishing it last night after we got home."

She opened a drawer in the dresser and brought out a bright red, knitted scarf. She stepped towards James, holding the two ends of it in her hands, then threw it over his head, around his neck, and pulled him towards herself,

"It's been knitted with love and I want you to feel my love wrapped around you whenever you wear it." She tucked the ends into a knot and pulled them together so that it was tight round his neck. Then she gave him a brief kiss on the cheek. He drew her into his arms. "Thank you," he said. "I shall treasure it." He hugged her for a moment and then released her.

"You've been a tower of strength to me, too. I value your friendship more than I can say," he said. "But I don't want to do anything to spoil it. We need to keep it in proper boundaries, do you understand what I mean?"

"I understand," she said.

✳✳✳

The chapel was crowded on the Sunday evening for the main annual carol service.

"This will be a strange Christmas for us all," James said, when the time came for the sermon. "The promise of peace on earth sounds hollow and distant amid the sounds of warfare. Many of you have hearts full of grief as you face Christmas without loved ones who have been killed. Many more of us will have pain in our hearts because of loved ones who are away fighting and will not be able to take their place at the Christmas table. A few are worried about family members who are missing. Merry making and jollity seem hollow and inappropriate against the backdrop of the times we are going through. But we do have reason to celebrate, even in the midst of anxiety and grief.

"The prophet Isaiah tells us of a nation that was shaking in fear and dread at the threat of war. It was to that nation that he brought the promise 'A virgin shall conceive and bear a son and you shall call his name "Immanuel"—"God with us".' That's what we celebrate at Christmas—the God who came to dwell among us. The God who is there with us to help us through the awful times we are going through and the God whose kingdom will rule and who one day will establish peace, justice and righteousness throughout the world."

He went on to press home his conviction that peace on earth could only be achieved by peace in people's hearts— and that peace could only come as people returned to God.

He concluded by saying,

"I pray that each one of you will experience God's presence in whatever way you need it. Enjoy your holidays, and a very happy Christmas to you all!"

✻✻✻

The next morning James set off to spend Christmas with Matthew and Edward at Win's parents' home in Millborough. As he sat in the train, watching the countryside drift by, his thoughts wandered to the warm Christmas farewells he had been given first by Bethan and then by Mary. He had to confess that he had developed a deal of affection for each of them. Their affirmation gave him a warm inner glow and yet also induced a degree of fear. He felt he was skating on thin ice.

And then his thoughts turned to the boys. They had written to him every week since his last visit, though James suspected it may have been under some duress from Cecilia, Win's mother. The letters were mainly a diary of what they had been doing, though Matthew had said in one of his letters that he was missing Win. James wondered where Win was and what she was doing—how she was coping with the chaos and tragedy of life on the front line.

The train pulled into the station at Millborough. As James put his head through the opened window to open the door, he saw Matthew and Edward running along the platform. Win's father, William, was walking behind them.

James crouched down and scooped the boys into his arms.

"I've missed you, It's lovely to see you again," he said, "and Edward, haven't you grown!"

"Guess what, Daddy?" Matthew said, "Grandpa's got a motor car!"

William caught up with them and greeted James warmly, holding James' hand with both of his.

"Great to see you, James!" he said.

"What's this about a motor car?" James said.

"I took delivery of it just a week ago. It's one of your Model T Fords, made in America. It's my Christmas present to myself."

William's ancestors for several generations had been blacksmiths. William himself had branched out into selling and repairing cycles and repairing other forms of machinery. He now had a chain of shops and workshops across the county and employed other people to do the manual work. Business had been going well. Horses were in short supply, many having been requisitioned for military service. People were buying bicycles instead and William had also benefited from contracts with the army to repair a variety of machinery. All in all, the business was prospering, he could well afford the car. But it was also an investment. William saw that there was a future in repairing motor vehicles. Owning one he could take apart and put together again was a step along the way.

It didn't take long to drive from the station to William and Cecilia's home near the river embankment, where Cecilia had prepared a sumptuous evening meal. James spent time with the boys, read them a chapter of a story and saw them off to bed .

"It's so lovely to see them again," James said as he returned to join Cecilia and William in the lounge. "You've been looking after them so well, I really do want to thank you for all you are doing for them and your generosity in funding them to go to the school."

"It's been a pleasure to have them and they are a credit to you and Win, Cecilia replied."

"Having had all girls it's nice to have boys to do some man things with," agreed William. "How are things in Oakdale? He added.

"Very busy," James said. "There are so many bereaved families and so many who are worried about their lads at the front. I'm giving some help once a week to a lady who is running a farm single handed while her husband is in the navy. He was involved in that business at Coronel and may have gone down with his ship – they haven't found a body. Poor woman doesn't know if he's alive or dead.

"At least the animosity to my pacifist principles has died down. I think, now people are being faced with the horror of war, they are seeing my point of view a bit more. In one sense I think it would be safe to have Edward and Matthew back home with me if you feel you've had enough of them?"

"We love having them here," William butted in, quickly. "They've got settled in the school now and made some good friends. It seems a shame to disrupt their lives again."

"We were going to ask if you could have them for the Easter and Summer holidays, though, Cecilia added."

"That would be splendid," James agreed, "And once again, thank you for your generosity towards them."

He went on to enquire whether they had heard anything from Win. It seemed they had received a letter from her at the same time as James and were not able to add anything to what he knew.

"I gather that the two of you made your peace before she left for the front?" William asked.

"To a degree, yes," James answered. "She still didn't see eye to eye with me where my pacifist views were concerned but she was more understanding. We didn't really have time to re-establish an ongoing peace though. I still love her and miss her terribly. I'm proud of her for going off to be a nurse at the front. I hope when this war is over we can create a harmonious home again."

"Win has always had a stubborn streak." William said. "And I have some sympathy with your point of view. If I didn't, I'd be off with the army myself."

"That's kind of you to say so," said James. "I was afraid you would think badly of me for not seeing eye to eye with your daughter."

The next few days were taken up with Christmas preparations – James went out in the car with William to fetch a fir tree from a local farm. On Christmas Eve William and James and the boys decorated the tree and the house, while Cecilia worked away in the kitchen, from which wafted a whole range of interesting cooking and baking smells.

On Christmas Day James took the boys to a service at the River Street Chapel. This was a congregation which met in a fine, Regency building and which, like Union Chapel in Oakdale, belonged to the same two historic free church denominations. It snowed overnight and, on Boxing Day, he took the boys out of town to some nearby hills where they were able to go tobogganing.

The holiday came to an end all too soon. James stayed to see the New Year in with them and then set off back to Oakdale on Friday 1st January, 1915.

***

The train passed through Bedford on the way. Looking out of the carriage and reading the station sign, James thought of the town's most famous citizen, John Bunyan, the author of *Pilgrim's Progress*. That gave him an idea for his sermon the following Sunday.

Chapter 20
1915

True Valour

Throughout the New Year celebrations James had again and again heard people expressing the hope that 1915 would see happier times and an end to the hostilities. He was unable to share that optimism. All the signs were that a stalemate was developing with huge forces amassed on each side with little hope of one side being able to quickly outfight the other. And yet, he felt he needed to offer some hope and encouragement in his New Year sermon.

He chose John Bunyan's famous hymn, "Who would true valour see" for the congregation to sing before the sermon and took it as the launch pad for what he had to say. John Bunyan's famous book, *Pilgrim's Progress*, allegorises the life of a believer in the story of Christian's journey from the City of Destruction to the safety of the Celestial City.

"Each of us is on a journey." He said. "A journey in which we meet many adventures and troubles and griefs and sorrows. These can either destroy us or make us stronger, depending on whether we approach them with faith and courage, or with doubt and anger. I don't know what you are going to encounter on your journey this year and I can't promise that this year will be any better than the last. All I can say is that God is there to help you. Each of us, in the words of Bunyan's hymn, has to be valiant.

Each of us can continue on the journey, through the troubles, if we keep our faith in God and our eyes on the goal of reaching heaven."

"Thank you James, that was very encouraging," Mary said as she left the church, "Shall I see you as usual on Friday?"

"You will indeed," James reassured her.

It was a brave attempt to give the congregation hope and strength to go on but, when he reflected on the sermon at home afterwards, he felt his words were hollow and feeble against the enormity of the situation facing the country as a whole and particular people in the congregation.

✳✳✳

The following morning a letter came from Win.

"I'm sorry not to have written earlier," the letter began and then continued:

> "I feel that my feet have not touched the ground since I arrived here. Each day we work long shifts to care for the wounded and the dying. At the end I'm so exhausted I just collapse into bed.

> "It's heart-rending to see the terrible injuries that some of the men are suffering—I say, "men" but most of them are just boys, really—arms and legs smashed to pieces, blinded, deafened by explosions, suffering terrible burns, their insides damaged by gunfire, I've seen it all. War reduces strong young men to whimpering babies crying for their mother. I've sat by young men who were dying and held their hand and wiped their brow. It reminded me of

how I sat by our boys' bedside when they were ill or they had had a nightmare. I miss the boys so much. I hope they are behaving themselves for Mama and Papa.

"James, I have to say you were right about how terrible war is. How could I ever have been taken in by the stupid false patriotism that was around when the war started.

"Having said that, there have been lighter moments. Many of the men keep their sense of humour and laugh and joke even when they are in pain. The other day a poor soldier tripped over a dead mule lying in the road, hit his head and suffered concussion. He was picked up by the men who were driving round collecting up the dead bodies. He woke up in the morgue and shook the corpses on either side of him, asking them for a light. He couldn't understand why they didn't answer. Eventually a young orderly came in bringing in body in from the hospital. The soldier sat up and asked for a cigarette. The poor orderly got the fright of his life and ran out as pale as a sheet!

"One day this war will be over and we can be together again. I hope your work in the chapel is going well. Please remember me to the congregation. I was sorry to hear of the attempt to have you ousted and apologise if my attitude made that situation worse. I think of you and the boys often and remember you in my prayers.

With my fondest love,

Win

James wiped a tear from his eye as he finished reading it. The days when he and Win had put the boys to bed together seemed a distant memory.

***

On the Friday, James cycled out to Sandybrook Farm as usual. He helped with the milking but then there was nothing more that Mary needed him to help with. They had breakfast in the farm kitchen. The children were there as the school term hadn't yet begun. They went off to play once the meal was over. James and Mary washed up and then sat at the table with a mug of tea each.

There was a moment of silence and then Jacob said,

"I had a letter from Win the other day."

"How is she?' Mary asked. James summarised the contents of her letter.

"You're lucky to know she's alright! I keep wondering if Jacob is dead or alive and, if he is alive, what he could be doing."

"It must be awful for you – not knowing." Said James.

"Apparently, I have to wait seven years before I can apply to the coroner to have him declared dead." Until then I can't do anything with his property. I'm tied to the farm. And I couldn't marry, if I found someone else."

James nodded, sympathetically.

"There's only one other person I could see myself marrying, anyway and his wife is still alive. I try not to wish anything ill towards her but... No, I'm sorry, I mustn't go down that road."

"Are you thinking, 'you and me?' "James guessed. "I know what you mean," he said. "I have to confess that a similar thought has crossed my mind before and I've had to push it out. You're right, let's not go down that road. Put a gate across it with a padlock. And a sign that says 'no entry.' It leads to confusion and hurt for us and for our children.'

He paused and they both sat in silence for a moment. Then James spoke again.

"The trouble is, I think we might still end up leaning on the gate together and looking over at the view."

Mary smiled and looked James in the eye.

"Looking at the view together helps," she said. "It's a nice view, even if we never go there."

"So long as we don't discuss it." James added. She nodded.

Chapter 21
1936

Getting Closer

Tuesday turned out to be a lovely, sunny day without a cloud in the sky. Awena and Heulwen went for a walk in the morning, following the banks of the brook as it meandered through the meadows to the west of the town. After an early lunch in the Red Lion, they returned to the guest house and waited in the hallway. Exactly on the dot of 2.00pm they heard a car horn outside and went to the door to see David waving to them from inside a burgundy coloured Austin 7.

"Now, the question is," David asked, once they had greeted one another, "Who's going to go in the back?"

"We both could," said Heulwen, immediately, to obviate the possibility of Awena being in the front with David while she was obliged to sit behind them.

"Let's toss for it," Awena suggested.

"Good idea!" Agreed David, and whoever loses the toss comes in the front coming home." He took out a coin and tossed it, Awena called "heads!" and won the toss. Reluctantly, Heulwen climbed into the back. David ebgaged the gears, did a quick turn in the road and then sped off through the town and out to the farm.

When they had bumped their way along the track to the farm and then come to a halt in the farmyard, a slim, petite lady who looked to be around 60 years old came to the door of the farm, wiping her hands on her apron.

"This is my Mum, Mary" David explained, and then, to his mother, "These are the young Welsh ladies I was telling you about."

"I'm very pleased to meet you.", his mother responded. "Welcome to Sandybrook Farm. I hope you are enjoying your holiday."

"I'm going to show them round first, mother," David told Mary, "... and we'll go for a bit of a walk up to the top of the hill. Then when we come back we'll have some tea."

"Alright then, I'll see you later," Mary called, and went back into the farm house.

"My Mum's amazing!" David said. She's a fantastic cook, always doing things to help people. She ran the farm practically on her own during the Great War and then again after my father died. And she brought up three of us children as well. Come this way and I'll show you around."

David led them around the farm buildings, eagerly reminiscing about childhood experiences as he did so. As a country girl herself, Heulwen seemed immediately at home in the setting of the farm, making a fuss of the cows and their calves, admiring the chickens and making friends with David's border collie and the farm cat.

"Have you not thought of raising sheep?" she said. "They'd do well in a hilly area like this."

"It's always been a dairy farm," David said, "I know where I am with cows. But I'll give your suggestion some thought. Thank you."

When they had done the tour of the farm buildings, David took them out for a walk in the fields. "I still can't get used to you being Miss Jones's niece," David said, as they walked three abreast across one of the pasture fields."

"Well, actually, David, I haven't told you the full story," Heulwen said, panting slightly with the exertion of walking briskly uphill. "The fact is, I called her my auntie, and until recently, I thought she was my auntie. But she died recently and, after she died, I found out she was really my Mam. Apparently she got herself in the family way, while she was teaching here. She came back to Wales to avoid the scandal. She had a married sister that had been unable to have children, so she gave me to her sister who adopted me. So she was my auntie in name but in reality she was my Mam."

"Golly, that discovery must have been a bit of a shock," David observed. "But that means you are actually my favourite teacher's daughter."

"I think you mean 'the daughter of my favourite teacher'," Awena said, by way of correction, "unless you know lots of teacher's daughters and Heulwen is your favourite among them!"

"I stand corrected," David agreed with a smile. "But if I did know lots of teachers' daughters, I could quite see you being the favourite, very easily."

Heulwen blushed. "That's nice of you to say so," she responded, and then continued, "The reason we came to Oakdale was not just to find out more about my Auntie's life here, but to see if we could find out who my biological father might be."

"Do you have any clues?" David asked.

Awena butted in. "The only thing we have to go on is a letter that Heulwen found in her auntie—her mother's—possession. It's from someone who might have been the man in question, though it's not conclusive. Whoever the man was, he seems to be apologising for some inappropriate behaviour. And he simply signed it "James"".

"James Wortley!" David said, immediately. "I bet it was him. I remember coming back into a classroom after school one day to collect something I'd left behind. He and your mum were standing close together in a corner. I could swear they were embracing each other and stepped apart when they heard me coming—but it happened very quickly and I told myself I was imagining things".

"Was he one of the other teachers?" Awena inquired.

"No, he was the minister of the chapel." David explained. But that meant he was also chairman of the school management committee. I say, do you mind if I tell mother about all this? She knew both of them. Rev Wortley was a friend of our family. When my Dad went off to sea during the great war, Rev Wortley used to come and help Mum out with the farm work one day a week."

Heulwen began to tremble inside. Coming to Oakdale to try to trace her father had been Awena's idea. She'd gone along with it, not actually expecting to have any success. Suddenly the idea was taking on a reality. She had a possible name for her father and a profession for him. She was standing in front of someone who might have actually known him. She had a sinking feeling inside which was a mixture of her own feelings—things were getting out of her control—and the feelings Bethan must have had. She started to sense how her mother would have felt, slipping into a love relationship with a married man who was a significant figure in the local community.

David and the two young women reached the top of a hill with a beautiful view across a shallow valley to the farm and some hills in the distance. They stood admiring the view while David continued talking.

"… his boys used to come and play at the farm. I got on really well with his son, Matthew. I'm still in touch with him, in fact. They all moved down south to Millborough in the end and Rev Wortley got a job as a teacher at a school there."

Not only was she learning real facts about her father, she apparently had a brother!

"How many children did this man have?" she asked.

"Just two," David said. "Matthew's brother is called Edward." He stopped, thought for a moment and said,

"Gosh, I suppose, if he is your father, then you have two half brothers."

Heulwen's legs were feeling so weak with emotion that she had to sit down. She plopped herself onto a tussock of grass.

"Excuse me, I just need to get my breath back," She said. "It's a bit much to take in."

"Are you alright?" Awena asked.

"Yes, don't worry, I'll be fine in a minute," she smiled.

"Would you like to meet Rev Wortley and his family?"
David asked.

"It would be very scary," she mused. "They might not want to
meet me."

"There's only one way to find out," said David. "As I say, I'm still
in touch with Matthew. I could help you make a contact with him
and we could see where we go from there."

"Maybe. Give me chance to think about it first," she said. Then,
"I'm OK now, can you help me up?" David reached out and took
her hand and pulled her into an upright position.

✳✳✳

When they reurned to the farm, Mary had prepared tea for them
with piles of sandwiches and home baked cake. They sat around
the table, drinking tea and eating. David started to ask his mother
probing questions about Rev Wortley and Miss Jones. Mary
started to look a little uncomfortable.

"Why are you asking me all this, David?" she asked.

Well, Heulwen, here, is the daughter of Miss Jones who used to
teach me at school. She's been brought up thinking that Miss
Jones was her aunt, but Miss Jones died recently and afterwards
Heulwen found out that the lady she thought was her aunt was
really her mother."

"Yes," Heulwen agreed and explained how she had found out the
truth. "I came here on holiday with my friend Awena to see if we
could find out any clues to the identity of my real father."

David butted in, "We've been putting two and two together and it

seems very probable to me that Heulwen's real father was
Rev Wortley.

Mary flinched visibly as David conveyed this information and
explained the letter that Heulwen had found.

"Excuse me a moment," she said. She got up from the table and
ran quickly upstairs.

It was a good ten minutes before she came down again.

"I'm sorry, I didn't mean to be rude," she said, "I just came over
a bit light-headed."

Once the meal was over and everyone was pitching in with the
washing up, Mary took Heulwen to one side and asked, "Do you
mind if I have a private word with you?" She took Heulwen into
the parlour.

"I think you must have seen that I was unsettled when David was
talking about your mother and Rev Wortley. Rev Wortley is a
lovely man. If he did turn out to be your father it would be
something to be very proud of. He was very brave and took a
stand against the war when it started. He worked really hard and
was a wonderful pastor and brought a lot of comfort to everyone
in the congregation during those dark years of the war. And I
have to confess to you that I worshipped the ground he walked
on. I really loved him. When my Jacob went off to the war, Rev
Wortley promised him that he would look out for me. He used to
come and help on the farm one day a week while my Jacob was
away and we got quite close. I had a feeling that Bethan Jones
felt much the same way towards him as I did. He was the chair of
the school management committee so they must have had
opportunity to spend time together…"

Heulwen interrupted,

"It must have been a shock to you then when David told you about our suspicions. I'm so sorry." She said.

"I felt a whole mixture of emotions," Mary explained. "I had a shot of jealousy at the thought that Bethan and he might have been so close—that maybe she knew him in a way I didn't…"

"My mother was a very determined lady," Heulwen said. "He might have found her hard to resist."

"I'd had the same thought," agreed Mary. "But the other emotion I had was joy at seeing you. There is something in your eyes and your manner that reminds me of James. It was like seeing him again. You are very, very, welcome here my dear. I'm genuinely pleased to meet you."

They paused in a silence where their eyes spoke to each other. Then Mary found her voice again.

"I've been very honest with you…"

She held out her hands in a welcoming gesture. Heulwen responded and yielded to her hug."

❋❋❋

When it was time to return home in the evening, Heulwen took her place in the front seat of David's car. "I've been thinking about what you said about contacting Matthew," she said as David drove them back to town. We can't be absolutely certain that he and I do have the same father. And it could be a big shock to him to find out that his father had done something—you know—wrong."

"You're right." David agreed, I don't think we should come out with the whole story straightaway. But how would you feel if I arranged a situation where you could meet him, socially, without him having to know who you are?"

"How could you do that?" Heulwen asked.

"I have an idea," He replied. "I'll tell you later."

When they arrived back at the guest house, David turned round to Awena in the back seat and said,

"Awena, I wonder if you'd mind awfully if I had a private chat with Heulwen before I leave?"

"Alright," Awena agreed. "I'll go on in and leave you."

David quickly hopped out and went round to hold the door open for her as she got out. "Thank you for a lovely afternoon," she said.

"I'd like to take you both out to show you some other local beauty spots if that's alright," he said. "Thanks for letting me have a moment with Heulwen."

Awena nodded and disappeared into the guest house. David slipped back into the driving seat and then turned to face Heulwen.

"Supposing I had a promising new lady friend and I really wanted all my friends to meet her because I was so proud of her, and supposing I wrote to my old friend Matthew and said, 'I and my new lady friend are passing through and would like to call on you ...'?"

"I'm not sure what you're saying?" Heulwen hesitated slightly as she spoke.

"If you were my girlfriend, it would be natural to set up a meeting with Matthew without him having to know about any blood relationship between you and him."

"But it would be wrong just to pretend…" Heulwen observed.

"Of course," David said. "I'm not suggesting we pretend. I'm saying I've enjoyed getting to know you, I'd like to get to know you more, I'd like to have a special relationship with you. Irrespective of getting to know Matthew. Can I start courting you?"

Heulwen was speechless for a moment.

"Please say 'yes'," David prompted her.

"Well, yes," she said. "Yes, please" Her eyes shone with excitement.

"May I seal it with a kiss?" David asked.

Heulwen leaned forward and he gave her a lingering kiss on the lips.

"I think Awena might be a bit envious!" Heulwen said, as she stepped out of the car.

"If she's a good friend she'll be pleased for you." David said, and kissed her again.

***

Heulwen burst into their room, her face radiant and smiling.

"He just kissed me!" she gasped. "Oh, Please be happy for me."
"Lucky you!" said Awena. "Of course, I'm pleased for you."

"He wants to take us out to see some of the local beauty spots
while we're here." He's calling for us tomorrow morning."

"I shall have to be content to be a gooseberry for the week then,"
Awena replied.

"If it works out, you can be my chief bridesmaid," Heulwen said.

"Let's take one step at a time." Awena replied. "Come here, I'm
so pleased for you. Let me give you a hug."

Chapter 22
1915

A happy New Year

On the Thursday of the first week of term, James called round to Bethan's cottage for their usual, weekly teatime meeting. His heart was racing and his palms sweating slightly as he knocked at the door. He wasn't sure if it was wise to be calling on her at home. The memory of the kiss under the mistletoe was fresh in his mind and he had a mixture of trepidation and excitement.

Bethan opened the door, welcomed him in and held out a hand to shake his.

"Happy New Year, James," she said. "It's nice to see you again; did you have a pleasant holiday?"

"Yes, thank you," James replied. "Bethan, there is something I need to say before we go any further."

"I know!" Bethan said, with a big smile. "That kiss under the mistletoe. You are going to tell me off and say it must never happen again."

"Well…" James began.

"It was very forward of me, I realise it put you in a difficult position. I can't bring myself to apologise because it was very, very, nice and I don't regret it at all but I promise I will never, ever put you in that position again. I give you my solemn word that from now on I will behave to you in a totally professional way."

She looked him in the eye with her lips pursed and the hint of a smile escaping from the corner of her mouth.

"Well, let's say no more about it," said James. And thank you for the book. I've been reading it over Christmas. How have the first few days of term gone?"

They continued their conversation, covering various matters to do either with the school or the chapel and parted with a handshake when James was ready to go.

Bethan kept her word and, each time they met from that point on, she behaved impeccably towards him. There was, however, one conversation which made him feel slightly uncomfortable.

"What are your views about polygamy?" she asked, out of the blue, at one of their Thursday teatime meetings.

James stammered slightly as he gathered his thoughts. "Well, that it's wrong, I suppose," James answered. "Why do you ask?"

"A little boy asked me about it in class the other day. He'd noticed that a lot of the men in the Old Testament had more than one wife – Abraham, Jacob, David, Moses, to name a few. I'd never thought about it before. I just wondered what you thought?"

"Christian teaching on marriage is based on the account of Adam and Eve in the Garden of Eden," James responded. "That clearly visualises one man and one woman. Marriage is also supposed to be a reflection of the relationship of Jesus and the church. Jesus sees the church as one. He only has one bride, not several."

"And yet there are so many different churches," Bethan observed. "It must seem to Jesus as if he has lots of wives sometimes, all squabbling with each other!"

"You may have a point there," James agreed.

"I sometimes wish polygamy were allowed," Bethan observed. There are so few really decent men around and lots of them are being slaughtered in this awful war. It severely reduces the chances of someone like me being able to experience the love of a good man, or to have children, at least, not without becoming someone's mistress or a 'kept woman', with all the stigma that's attached to that. You know I'd love to be able to go to Win and say, 'Would you be willing to share James with me?' Just theoretically, supposing it was allowed and Win agreed, how would you feel about taking me on as a number two wife?"

"I'm only teasing you," She added quickly.

"I think there are too many 'ifs' there, anyway!" James exclaimed "...and I don't think it would be wise of me to answer!"

"I'm sorry, James," Bethan said, gently. "I'm being naughty again and I promised I wouldn't. Please forgive me."

"I'm flattered that you gave voice to the question," James replied. Of course I forgive you."

✳✳✳

The following day, James was sitting in the kitchen at Sandybrook Farm with Mary, when a knock came at the door. Mary answered it and came back clutching a brown envelope.

"James, can you open it, please?" she asked. "I'm all of a tremble. It must be about Jacob."

James took the envelope from her hands, opened it and read out,

"CPO Jacob Hollinshead was today reported alive aboard merchant ship heading Auckland, New Zealand."

Mary took it from his hands and read it for herself, in disbelief.

"He's alive!" She exclaimed

"Thank God!" James added. Before he left he knelt down in the kitchen with Mary and gave thanks for the good news.

✳✳✳

When James arrived at Sandybrook Farm on the first Friday in February, the two carthorses that Mary had borrowed for ploughing before Christmas were standing in the yard. Mary was standing by one of them, patting it on the nose and giving it a titbit.

"You're an 'andsome beast, en't you. my lover?" James heard her say. She hadn't noticed him creeping up behind her,

"Thank you for the compliment!" he said.

"Oh, James, I were talking to the horse, not you," she said. "I've

borrowed them again so that we can go and drill that field we
ploughed, to plant the seeds."

It was a bright, dry, sunny day and they worked together with the
horses for most of the day, working their way up and down the
field with the drilling machine that planted the seeds at the
correct depth and covered them over. At lunchtime they sat
together in a sunny spot against a hedge which shielded them
from the wind. They had a beautiful view and sat admiring it
together and pointing out various landmarks that they could see
in the distance.

"I was just thinking about that conversation we had about looking
at the view together but not going there," James said. I came
across a quotation the other day—from some Frenchman. He
said 'Being in love doesn't mean gazing into each other's eyes
but looking together in the same direction.' "

"Does that make us in love?" Mary asked.

"Maybe." James said. "It certainly means we have a precious gift
that needs to be treated with care."

✲✲✲

It was another couple of weeks before Mary received any more
news of Jacob. It came eventually in the form of a letter from
him. Mary made a special visit to town to report the news
to James.

In the letter Jacob explained that, after his ship had been sunk in
the engagement with a German flotilla at Coronel, he had ended
up in a lifeboat with two shipmates. The boat had some
emergency provisions but only one oar. This enabled them to
keep the craft head to the wind but not to make any progress.

They had drifted with the current northwards along the coast of South America and passed within sight of the Galapagos Islands.

After drifting for several weeks they were sighted and picked up by a steamship that was heading for New Zealand, having passed through the newly opened Panama Canal.

It took another couple of weeks to cross the Pacific. At last they reached Auckland and were able to make contact with the Admiralty. They were instructed to join the crew of a troopship bringing soldiers from New Zealand until such times as a convenient transfer could be arranged to a Royal Naval vessel.

"It could still be a good while before he gets back home, Mary said to James, "But at least he's alive."

Chapter 23
1915

Easter Holidays

Winter turned to spring, and James continued with his regular weekly routine, taking the services at the chapel on Sunday, spending mornings in his study, afternoons visiting members of the chapel congregation, giving special attention to the elderly and the families of the men who had already been killed or injured in the war. The evenings would either be given to committee meetings of one kind or another or further pastoral visits. On Thursday afternoons he took afternoon tea with Bethan Jones to discuss the affairs of the school and then early on Friday morning he would cycle out to Sandybrook Farm to help Mary with whatever work needed doing. Saturday was an unpredictable day which might include conducting a wedding, or attending a regional meeting to do with either of the two denominations the chapel belonged to, or more pastoral work, or more last minute preparations for Sunday.

Letters came every week or fortnight from Win. James usually wrote back within a couple of days.

The Easter holidays brought a welcome change from the routine. On Monday, 29th March, James travelled down to Millborough to collect Edward and Matthew from Win's parents and to bring them home to stay for the Easter holidays.

As they travelled back together on the train, James began to realise how much the two boys had grown and matured, even since Christmas. Initially, when the visit was proposed, James had been anxious about how he would keep them occupied for the twelve days they were to stay with him. He soon realised that they were capable of making their own amusement and were now old enough to find their way around Oakdale unaided. They, in turn, remembered their old haunts from when they lived there before. The little town had plenty to offer young boys, including a park to play cricket, a fish pond where they could sail toy boats (when the water bailiff wasn't around) and various interesting places alongside the brook where dams could be built or tadpoles and minnows fished for. The cattle market was also a favourite place for them to visit with its constant hustle and bustle and the noise and smells of the various animals.

Mary had given James and the boys an invitation to visit the farm and to play with Hannah, David and Eleanor. They took advantage of the offer on the Wednesday after they arrived. David and Matthew immediately struck up a bond. Edward found himself pulled in two directions by Mary's girls. Hannah, who had a tomboyish streak, was continually inviting him to join in activities where she could show off that she was as good as any boy—climbing trees or racing through the fields. Eleanor also took a shine to Edward and drew him into a whole range of "let's pretend" games in which he co-operated obligingly.

The visit was so successful that James and Mary arranged for Mary's children to come to the manse one day and then for the two boys to go to the farm the next and so-on through the week. Not that James left the boys to their own devices—he joined in cricket games in the park with them on several occasions and also dusted the cobwebs off the croquet set and mowed the tennis court so that he and the children could make use of them. Having the boys with him lifted James's spirits and brought a sense of joy and enthusiasm which spilled over into his sermon on Easter Sunday which was based on a verse from 1 Peter chapter 1 v 3¬6 "...he has given us new birth into a living hope through the resurrection of Jesus Christ from the dead...wherein ye greatly rejoice, though now for a season, if need be, ye are in heaviness through manifold temptations."

However, when the boys returned to Millborough, the house felt unnaturally quiet and empty and James missed them as much as he had enjoyed having them with him. He shared his feelings with Mary when he saw her at the chapel on the Sunday morning after he had taken them back.

"It's been a lovely week, though, hasn't it?" said Mary. "I'm glad the children all got on so well together. It gave me the chance to see you more often."

"Yes, it felt as if we were a family together." James agreed.

The next day, James was surprised to receive a letter from Jacob. It had been sent from Malta.

He was now attached to a Royal Naval vessel, he said, which was in Malta for repairs after some damage incurred during the Gallipoli campaign.

The letter ended:

> "Thank you so much for keeping an eye on Mary and the children for me. I haven't told Mary but I am hoping to be home in the middle of June. I want it to be a surprise for her when I get back, so please don't tell her. I also haven't

told her that I have sustained an injury that means that, when I eventually get home, I will be invalided out of the navy so I will be home for good. I look forward to seeing you again in due course,

Your good friend,

Jacob."

Chapter 24
1915

A lovely surprise

It was a beautiful, sunny, Friday morning in the middle of
May. James cycled out to the farm as usual and began to help
Mary with the milking. As they were working together, she
called across the milking parlour, over the backs of the cows,

"I've something to show you, when we've finished here,"

"What's that?" James asked.

"A lovely surprise" she replied. But you'll have to wait and see."

When they'd finished the milking and had some breakfast, James
reminded her, "You said there was something you wanted to
show me?"

"There is," she said, "but we have to take a walk to find it."

They set off from the farmhouse, walking uphill through
the fields.

"Have you heard any more from Jacob?" James asked, as they
walked toghether.

"Yes," she said, "I had another postcard, from Malta this time. It said he was alright and the weather was nice. I suppose he couldn't say much more. They're not allowed to give any details of where they are heading, in case it gets into the wrong hands."

It was all James could do to stop himself blurting out the contents of the letter that he had received from Jacob. He felt torn between a loyalty to Mary which demanded that he told her and a loyalty to Jacob which demanded that he didn't. He made an indeterminate noise in his throat which indicated that he understood the inability of servicemen to talk about their plans in wartime and kept on walking in silence. Mary led the way to the field that they had ploughed and planted in the preceding few weeks.

"There's the surprise!" she said. "We did that together!"

The field was full of wheat, still a little green but starting to bleach in the sun. A mass of red poppies were growing among the wheat and especially around the edges of the field.

"You're right, It's amazing!" James agreed. Though it's not quite true to say 'We did it.' I think God had a part in it too."

"I know!" Mary responded. "But doesn't it make you feel proud?"

"It does indeed," said James. "And aren't the poppies beautiful?"

"They do thrive where the soil have been disturbed," Mary explained.

"I know," said James. "In one of her letters Win was telling me how the battlefields are full of poppies in Flanders."

He bent down and picked two poppies. He playfully pushed one into Mary's hair and then put the other into the buttonhole of his jacket.

"Thank you, kind sir!" she laughed and did a little curtsey. James looked at her from the side. She was smiling, her eyes dancing with pleasure and amusement. The wind gently lifted the locks of her hair. Standing against the background of the poppy-filled wheatfield and an azure blue sky, she looked a real picture—at home in her natural environment and thoroughly beautiful.

"I wish I could paint her and capture this moment for ever!" James thought to himself.

Chapter 25
1936

Couldn't be better

"It's been a lovely week. Thank you so much! I'm going to miss you."

Heulwen was leaning out of the carriage window. She reached down and kissed David again. He put his arms around her neck and held her as close as he could without actually dragging her out of the window.

"I love you so much. I'll write soon." He said. "I'm really looking forward to coming up to see you at the beginning of September. I've never been to Wales before."

"You'll love it," Heulwen said, "I promise."

The guard blew his whistle, jumped aboard and slammed his door. The locomotive began to hiss steam and slowly to set the train in motion. Awena came to the window too, and both girls waved. David waved back and continued waving until the train disappeared into the tunnel at the north end of the station.

Heulwen burst into tears as the train entered the tunnel.

"He's so lovely, I don't want to leave him!" She exclaimed, in between sobs.

✳✳✳

But three weeks later, Heulwen's emotions were quite reversed as she waited on another railway station platform in Bangor. Coincidentally the stations at both Oakdale and Bangor each have a tunnel at one end. her heart was racing with excitement as she watched for the express from London to emerge from the tunnel at the end of the platform.

As soon as the train came out of the tunnel, David was leaning out of the door of the very first carriage which, of course, then had to travel the whole length of the platform before it came to a halt. Heulwen ran along the platform after him. As he stepped out of the carriage and she reached him, David opened his arms and swept her into an enthusiastic embrace.

They caught a taxi to a guest house overlooking the Menai Straits where they had booked to stay for three nights. Heulwen had planned for them to spend a few days in Bangor so that she could show him the Normal College where she was training to be a teacher and some of her favourite places round about—among them the castles at Caernarfon and Biwmares, and Penmon Point with its views across the sea to the mountains. The following day they planned to make the journey to Hebron for him to meet Her Mam and Dad—she still called them Mam and Dad, she couldn't dishonour the love and care they had given her over the years by calling them anything else, even though she now knew they were really Auntie Louise and Uncle Tom. She and David would stay there a few days and then travel back to Bangor—Heulwen to start the first term of her final year at the College and David to catch the train back to Oakdale.

As soon as they were settled into their rooms, they went for a walk together, up to Roman Camp, with its amazing view over the Menai Straits, past the Normal College and the university arts building which dominated the town from the top of a steep hill. Heulwen was used to seeing the college and university buildings thronged with students—to find them almost deserted seemed odd. They came back to the guest house for an evening meal and then walked down to the long pier that jutted out into the straits, so far that its end is nearer to the other side than to the near shore. As the sun began to set, they came back, just as the pier was closing, and found a small public garden with a bench overlooking the water. They sat there together. A bed of rose bushes stood between them and a low, stone wall on the other side of which were the waters of the Straits. They lingered there, enjoying the fragrance of the roses and watching as the setting sun shed its rays onto the Anglesey shore, as the moon rose and the stars began to come out one by one. They listened to the soft whisper of the waves breaking on the shingle and, as the stars came out, identified the constellations—Orion, the Great and Little Bear, the Pleiades. It was a calm evening and the stars were reflected in the water.

"Isn't this lovely!" David said. "Couldn't be better!" Heulwen agreed and nestled her face into David's shoulder. Eventually, it got cold, so they went in—to their separate rooms, though it was a wrench to part.

The next day, as they sat eating a picnic lunch at Penmon Point, admiring the view towards the Snowdonia Mountains, James said,

"I've been in touch with Matthew, by the way. I've arranged to meet up with him in the last week of October. "I've told him I'm planning to take my new girlfriend on a trip to London and thought we'd stop off to see him on the way as we are passing through. I hope that's alright!"

"That's a convenient time to get away from college for a long weekend," said Heulwen. "But it will need to be a flying visit. If I come down to Oakdale on the Friday, we can go to Millborough the next day and on to London in the evening. We could spend the Sunday and Monday in London, then I'd have to get the train from Euston to come straight back to Bangor."

"Sounds good," said David. "Let's make that a date."

"It's going to be strange, though, seeing a stranger and thinking, 'He's almost certainly my brother!'"

"We can be honest about who your mother is." David said. "I think we just play it by ear as to how much we say."

David and Heulwen enjoyed the rest of the week together. David was amused and fascinated by hearing people speaking Welsh around him. He was blown away by the beauty of the North Wales countryside and immediately hit it off with Tom and Louise, having lengthy and impassioned discussions with Tom about the relative merits of sheep rearing and dairy farming.

The day before they returned to Bangor, Louise and Heulwen had some time together while David was out helping Tom bring some sheep back from the market.

"He's a lovely young man, *cariad*," Louise said. "Shame he's not Welsh, but he'll do. I doubt you'll find a better one."

"Yes, even if I don't find my real Dad, it looks like I might have found a husband!" Heulwen agreed, "Though it's early days. Let's not count our chickens before they've hatched!"

"I can't get over that he actually knew your Mam!" Louise replied.

"You mean Auntie B!" exclaimed Heulwen. "You'll always be Mam to me. Yes Auntie B was David's teacher. Sounds like he was a bit of a teacher's pet, too from what I've heard. But I haven't told you, we think we know who the man was that got Auntie B in the family way with me. We think it was the minister of the chapel in the town. David has been friends since childhood with his son and is arranging for me to meet him. He could be my half-brother!"

"Do be careful, my love," Louise warned. "You could cause a lot of hurt bringing out secrets or making accusations that might not be true."

"I realise that," Heulwen said, "I'm not wanting to start up a relationship with them, just to find out a little bit more about them."

Chapter 26
1915

A sudden storm

About 10.00 am on the Wednesday morning of the last week in June, James was in his study, clearing some correspondence and preparing to examine some papers that the local education authority had sent out to school management committees.

His concentration was interrupted by a loud knock at the door. He opened it to find Jacob standing outside.

"Hello, Pastor, I'm back!" he said, with a broad smile in a tanned and weather beaten face. He had a plaster cast on his left wrist. James stood for a moment, stunned, and then said,

"Jacob! Come in, It's good to see you! When did you arrive?"

"I got back home yesterday afternoon," Jacob replied.

James took Jacob into the kitchen and brewed a pot of tea, at moments asking him about his adventures and murmuring expressions of interest and encouragement as Jacob told his story.

"So, we arrived off the Dardanelles and met up with *HMS Inflexible*. The three of us were transferred over to the British vessel. But then a while later, we ran into a mine which damaged the ship's bows. There was 35 men killed by the explosion. I got some damage to my wrist, which is why I've got the plaster on it. I smashed it against the bulkhead when I was blown back by the blast. It's enough to get me invalided out, though. We were towed into Malta to have some temporary repairs done and then came back to Rosyth, arriving on Saturday – and here I am."

"Well I'm glad you got home safe and sound!" James said. "It's good to see you. Are you well enough to go back to work on the farm?"

"Oh, aye. Fortunately I'm right handed, so I can do most things," James said, confidently. "It just catches me now and then and I have to be careful not to put strain on it. Just as well, because it's haymaking time. We'll be busy for the next few weeks. The army doctor said it will never be 100% but it will gradually improve. I'm so grateful for all you've done while I've been away. Mary said she'd have been lost without you."

When Jacob left, James experienced a flat, empty, sinking feeling in his heart and his stomach.

He was glad for both Jacob and Mary that Jacob had arrived home safely. But James had grown to rely on Mary's companionship. The Fridays they had spent together had been precious—the one opportunity he had to let his guard down and to share his thoughts and feelings with someone understanding and trustworthy. Now Jacob was home, there would be no reason for him to visit Sandybrook Farm on Fridays. Jacob and Mary needed time together to restore their relationship. He would be an intrusion.

James began to feel very alone.

✳✳✳

The one source of companionship that James still had was
Bethan. It so happened that he and Bethan had an outing planned
and, over the course of a couple of days, the sadness he was
feeling about the necessary change in his relationship with Mary
began to be somewhat assuaged by anticipation of the
forthcoming outing with Bethan.

The local Baptist Association was to hold its annual meetings in a
town several miles along the railway line. James as minister and
Bethan as church secretary were both expected to be there, so
they arranged to travel together, meeting at the station in the
morning to catch the train. The whole week had been hot and
sunny and Saturday morning again dawned bright with not a
cloud in the sky. Both James and Bethan were dressed
appropriately for the fine weather. James was wearing a light
jacket and Bethan looked stunning in a full length, white, short
sleeved, summer dress with navy blue trimmings, a wide navy
blue sash and a row of four blue and white flowers sewn in a line
down the bottom of one side. A straw hat with matching flowers
and navy blue ribbon completed the effect, along with a navy
blue choker with a flower at the front and a small, navy
blue handbag.

They had a compartment to themselves on the way there and
spent the journey talking animatedly about the school, the chapel
and its congregation, the world, and the war. As usual, Bethan
was full of questions and eager and attentive to James' attempts
to answer them.

They sat together in the meetings, mingling in between sessions
with people from other chapels in the area.

The day ended with an early evening meeting that finished at about 7.00pm. James and Bethan left quickly as they had to hurry to the station to catch the train back. Near where they stood, waiting on the station platform in the evening sunlight, was a flower bed that was a mass of blue forget-me-nots.

"Look, aren't they beautiful!" Bethan observed.

"They are indeed," James agreed. "I love forget-me-nots. They are among my favourite flowers."

"Mine, too," agreed Bethan. "I shall always think of you now, whenever I see a forget-me-not."

"That's very kind of you", James responded.

"It's been a nice day," Bethan observed. "It has," James agreed and then added "I've enjoyed your company." At that moment the train came rumbling into the platform. James opened the door for Bethan and she stepped in. The train this time was quite full and they could not find a compartment to themselves but were forced to share one with other people. They sat opposite each other on the corridor side of the compartment, making little conversation but exchanging the occasional smile or the kind of knowing looks that often pass between people who have an affinity as they communicate their reactions to things going on around them, without having to say anything.

As the train drew near to Oakdale, the sky clouded over and became dark and that there were flashes of lightning in the distance. There was a loud clap of thunder as they walked across the bridge to reach the station entrance.

"I'll walk you home, Bethan, if that's alright?" James said.
"Thank you, I'd appreciate that," she replied.

They had barely walked a hundred yards from the station when huge spots of rain began to splash down from the sky. They quickened their steps but soon the heavy drops merged into a continuous, heavy downpour, while the flashes of lightning and claps of thunder became more frequent. They stopped for a moment under an archway at the entrance to one of the buildings but James observed, "I don't think this is going to stop in a hurry. Let's just run for it!" He took Bethan by the hand and together they ran the half mile or so to her cottage, arriving breathless but with faces glowing from the exertion and the coldness of the rain. By the time they got there they were both soaked to the skin,

Bethan fumbled in her handbag for the key, her breast heaving as she caught her breath. "James, you'd better come in to dry off, you're soaked," she panted, as she opened the door and then, not waiting for a reply, she pushed him in and closed the door behind them.

"There's some wood and coal by the fireplace and you'll find matches in the kitchen," she said, "Can you light a fire in the range and also in the parlour, James? I'll change out of these wet things and then bring you some towels and find you something to wrap yourself in while your clothes are drying."

She disappeared upstairs and James got to work. Soon he had fires blazing merrily in both the parlour fireplace and the range in the back room. He went through to the kitchen to wash the coal dust from his hands. As he finished he turned to find Bethan standing behind him. She was wearing a white satin peignoir and nightdress and had unpinned her long hair which hung freely around her shoulders and was still damp.

"I've brought you a blanket to put round you," she said. "Take off your wet things and I'll hang them up on the drying rack in the kitchen."

James hesitated.

"Don't worry, I have a brother and cousins, I've seen naked men before," she said, with a smile. "I'll go in the kitchen and cook us something to eat, while you're sorting yourself out. Let me just fill a kettle and put it on the range first."

James undressed and, with the help of his leather belt, he managed to fix the blanket around him in a way that provided some degree of modesty.

Bethan arranged their wet clothes on the wooden drying rack in the kitchen and hoisted it up to the ceiling on its pulleys.

"Go and sit by the fire, James," she said, "I'll prepare something for us to eat."

She cooked an omelette and served it with bread and a mug of warm tea. They sat at the table together. The thunder was now dying down to an occasional, distant rumble.

"It's nice not to be eating alone," Bethan observed.
"I know what you mean," James agreed.

The meal over, James began to gather the plates and cups and took them into the kitchen.

"You don't have to…" Bethan began. "No, let me…" he insisted. Bethan picked up a tea towel to dry up. When the last item had been dried and put away, they were left standing in the kitchen together, James wrapped in the blanket, Bethan looking beautiful with her long dark hair cascading over the white satin of the peignoir. James waited for an invitation from Bethan to go and sit in the parlour. Instead, she remained standing. She reached up to feel the ankles of James' trousers that were hanging down from the rack.

.

"Your things are still damp!" she said, "You can't go yet."

She remained standing, where she was. She seemed to be waiting for something. Her very stillness was magnetic, pulling James towards her. On an impulse, he reached out and took her into his arms.

She didn't resist but stayed still in his embrace with her hands at her side.

"I'm being good James, like I promised," she said and then she leaned against his chest and exclaimed,

"James, I love you so much!"

James began to feel a wave of desire wash over him. He tightened his embrace and sought out her lips. They kissed, tentatively at first and then with passion, holding each other close together. Bethan's hand parted the blanket and began to caress the skin of his chest. They stood there for minutes, intense desire sweeping over them. Then Bethan took his hand and began to walk slowly backwards. She drew him with her and he followed, out of the kitchen, through the living room, into the hallway and up a flight of stairs.

"I mustn't do this, this is wrong!" James thought to himself as he found himself in her bedroom. He was about to object and then Bethan undid the peignoir, let it fall to the floor and then lifted her nightdress over her head so that she was standing naked in the dim light that shone through the curtains from a street lamp outside. She gently pushed the blanket from James's shoulders and then hugged him to her. He could feel the softness of her breasts against his chest, the warmth of her thighs against his. Her hands continued to caress his body. Then she kissed him again and drew him down with her onto the bed.

Something snapped inside James. All the pressure to be a perfect example to the community, all the tension of opposing the war when everyone was in favour of it, all the strain of the disagreement with Win, all the frustration of holding back his feelings for Mary, all of the pressure he had been under erupted in one moment of angry rebellion and he pushed the voice of his conscience aside, taking comfort in Bethan's embrace. For a moment his loneliness seemed to evaporate as their bodies joined, moving together in a slow, intense undulation until they each reached their moment of release.

Almost as soon as their lovemaking was over a feeling of shame and guilt swept over James but he felt instinctively that it would be hurtful to Bethan if he were to move. He stayed lying in her arms. She caressed his head and hair. "That was wonderful," she said. They continued, lying in each other's arms until they fell asleep.

Chapter 27
1915

Sunday morning

When James woke up it was still dark outside. Everything was quiet and still. An owl hooted in the distance. James slipped out of bed, as quietly as he could. He could dimly make out Bethan's body in the moonlight. She was lying there, naked and still fast asleep. He tiptoed downstairs. His clothes were dry now. He quickly got dressed, went out, closing the door behind him as gently as he could, and walked home through the deserted streets. As he walked, the first light of dawn began to brighten the eastern horizon and all the birds in the surrounding trees began to celebrate the start of a new day in the dawn chorus. Rather than enjoying the sound as he might normally do, James resented it. It seemed as if all of nature were mocking him for his hypocrisy and weakness.

It was already Sunday morning. In a few hours he would need to be leading the service at the chapel. He felt totally unworthy to do it but there was no way out of it. He managed a couple of hours of disturbed sleep before making himself some breakfast and starting to get ready. His prayers were full of remorse as he prepared to set off for the chapel.

Trembling inside and deeply conscious of his hypocrisy, he mounted the pulpit steps to lead the service. As he looked around the congregation he realised with gratitude that Bethan was not there. Mary and Jacob and their three children were sitting together in their usual pew.

The sermon James had prepared was about the mercy and forgiveness of God. He felt keenly the bitter irony of the familiar words from Isaiah's prophecy that he had chosen, days ago, for this morning's reading:

> "Come now, and let us reason together, saith the Lord: though your sins be as scarlet, they shall be as white as snow; though they be red like crimson, they shall be as wool."

He linked it with St Paul's words, "While we were yet sinners, Christ died for us."

He had preached on those passages before and had often drawn them to the attention of people whose consciences had been troubling them. But this was the first time he felt the full weight of the words. Brought up in a God fearing family he had never done anything really wrong, other than an occasional white lie or loss of temper and entertaining thoughts that he would be ashamed of if others were aware of them. Now he read the words as someone who had substantially and deliberately broken one of God's commandments. The guilt seared his heart. Tears came to his eyes and his voice choked as he spoke of God's mercy—the mercy that he himself so desparately needed.

The sermon was followed by communion when tiny glasses of wine and pieces of bread were passed around the congregation to remind them of Jesus Christ's atoning death, his body broken and his blood poured out as an offering for sin, God taking on himself the punishment that human beings deserve so that he could justly forgive them.

"Father, I really am not worthy to be sitting here," he prayed inwardly, as the organ played softly and the deacons walked up and down the chapel, passing out the plates and trays of cups, "…but please have mercy on me."

✻✻✻

He sat alone in his study in the afternoon, his thoughts and feelings tumbling in a confused circle, swinging between fear and guilt and shame. At times he also experienced an intruding enjoyment of his memory of holding Bethan in his arms—a feeling that kept pushing its nose into his conciousness as hard as he tried to push it away. Eventually he wrote a letter to Bethan:

> "My dear Bethan,
>
> I am so ashamed about what has happened. I despise myself for my weakness. I should have behaved more responsibly. Please understand that nothing of the kind must ever happen again. At the same time I would like to assure you that, however wrong it was, I cannot remember it with anything but joy and gratitude. I shall always cherish the memory of those precious moments and you will always have a special place in my heart. I am, as you will realise, in your power. You now have the wherewithal to destroy my life. Please look kindly on my plea to be discreet and spare me the terrible consequences should what passed between us be widely known—consequences that would also not be pleasant for you. Let us try to be strong and act responsibly when we see each other again.
>
> With fondest regards from James."

He walked round to Bethan's cottage after the evening service. He was planning to put the letter through her letterbox. When he got there it seemed cowardly and distant.

Instead. he knocked at the door. Bethan opened, greeted him with a beaming smile and invited him in.

"I was just going to leave you a letter, but I wanted to make sure you are alright, he said." He tried to express in words what he had already written. The light in Bethan's eyes died away and the smile began to fade from her face as he spoke.

"I'm alright, James," Bethan responded, when he had finished speaking. "I think you are more racked with guilt than I am. That's why I stayed away from church this morning, to make it easier for you. I've spent some precious hours in the arms of the man I love. If I never feel your embrace again, at least I can remember those moments with joy and pleasure. I don't want to take you from your family or to cause any more difficulties for you. One part of me wants to continue a secret affair with you but I guess that's not really a possibility."

She walked towards him and gave him a kiss on the cheek. It was a dangerous moment. Everything in him ached to take her in his arms again. But he stepped backwards, handed her the letter and whispered, "God bless you."

Then he turned and walked swiftly to the door.

Three weeks later, it was the end of the school term. In those three weeks Bethan didn't come to the services at the chapel. James put an end to their weekly tea time meetings. They saw each other, briefly, at the end of term assembly. With other people around and within earshot, they politely wished each other a good vacation.

Chapter 28
1936

Even though he die

Heulwen hurried down the stairs into the entrance hall and skipped across to the pigeon hole where students collected their mail. She took out the pile from the "H" section"and sorted through all those addressed to "Hughes". A smile broke out on her face as she spotted the one with David's writing and an Oakdale postmark.

Pressing it to her lips, she ran back up the stairs to her room to open it. Since the start of the term, David had written to her and she had replied every day.

"My Darling,

"I have some bad news for you," David's letter began.

He went on to report that he had received a letter from Matthew, explaining that Rev Wortley had been taken ill. He was in hospital with tuberculosis and his family were afraid for his life.

Later in the day, she shared the news with Awena. "They must be so worried and sad," Awena said "– and you, too of course."

"It will be a big disappointment to me if I don't get to see him before he dies," Heulwen agreed, "but it's selfish of me to feel that. If I'd known him I would feel the loss more keenly. I keep praying for Mr Wortley and his family."

A few days later, one of the college porters knocked at her door in the afternoon with a telegram that had just arrived. Heulwen opened it and read it.

> Rev Wortley died + funeral Tues + Hollinsheads going + you come too? + David

Heulwen skipped a couple of lectures to walk to the railway station to check train times and then back to the post office to send a telegram in reply;

> Coming too + arrive Oakdale station Mon 3.30pm + love Heulwen.

"I've nothing to wear!" She exclaimed to Awena when she told her. The outfit she had worn from Auntie B's funeral was back at home in Hebron. It would be a long trek to go there to fetch it, so she and Awena spent the Saturday frantically shopping in Bangor to fit her out with cothes that were suitable to wear at a fiuneral. On the Monday morning she set off early to catch the train.

❋❋❋

Heulwen put her head out of the window as soon as the train emerged from the tunnel into Oakdale station. David was there waiting and waving. He ran over, opened the door for her and helped her down onto the platform and into his arms.

"I've missed you so much!" he exclaimed. "It's lovely to see you again." Carrying her case in one hand and holding her hand with the other, he led her out into the station yard where his Austin 7 was waiting.

"We're all going down to the funeral," he explained, as he stowed Heulwen's case in the back of the car. So you'll have the pleasure of meeting my brother and sister."

"Oh, do pile on the pressure!" she said. I'm nervous as it is about meeting Rev Wortley's family."

"I'll introduce you as my fiancée," he said. "That's enough of a reason for you to be there. If you like you can explain who your mother was. They'll know that she knew Rev Wortley as a colleague. That's gives you another reason reason for being there. A funeral's not a time for bringing skeletons out of cupboards."

"I know," she said, "but the thought of meeting them still makes me nervous."

Heulwen was bowled over by the welcome she received as she arrived at Sandybrook farm. Mary ran out to welcome her as soon as David's car drew up outside the front door.

"Heulwen, I'm so pleased to see you again!" she said, hugged her and kissed her on the cheek.

David introduced her to Hannah, who was taller than Heulwen but could have been taken for her sister, with her black curls and curvaceous figure. Heulwen noticed her wedding ring and remembered David had told her that she was married and had a son. Heulwen asked after her husband and child and Hannah explained that they had stayed at home. Eleanor was slimmer and more petite, with her mother's grey-green eyes.

"You have to be a very special person to win Davie's affections," she said, "I've been trying to pair him off with one or other of my friends for years."

To begin with, Heulwen felt ill at ease with the whole family there together. But as the evening wore on she relaxed and began to feel more and more at home. "I love the way you speak, it's so sweet," said Eleanor. "Is it true what David says, that you didn't learn English until you were six?"

"That's normal where I come from," she said. David pitched in. "When I travelled on the bus and the little narrow gauge train to get to Heulwen's village, everyone else was chattering away in Welsh and I was the only person who couldn't understand a word, It really is a foreign country, believe me."

"We're going to catch the 7.52 train in the morning," David explained, as the evening drew to a close. That will give us time to get some lunch somewhere before the service which is at 2.00pm in the Riverside chapel. We'll get a train back about six."

Mary showed Heulwen to her room.

"I remember when your father came to Oakdale, we put him up overnight and he slept in this very same bed," she said. "A lot of water 'ave passed under the bridge since then."

❋❋❋

They arrived at the chapel in good time and took their seats towards the back. The organ was playing softly. Mary looked round with interest at the beautifully proportioned regency building with its rectangular, clear glass windows and balcony wrapped around three sides of the sanctuary.

Suddenly, the undertaker's voice boomed out behind her,

"Will you all please stand?" The minister's voice began to recite verses of from the Bible in a solemn voice.

> "I am the resurrection and the life. He that believes in
> me, though he die, yet shall he live."

Heulwen recognised the same verses that had been read out at the
beginning of Auntie B's funeral—her Mam's funeral, only a few
months before, except now they were in English, instead of
Welsh. It dawned on her for the first time that she was half
English—she had been so proud of her Welsh heritage, the
realisation came as something of a shock.

The men bearing the coffin passed her. "He's in there!" she
thought to herself. "This is the closest I will ever get to the man
who gave me life. If only I could hve met him when he
was alive!"

Then she became aware of a grey haired lady, dressed in black,
who was walking behind the coffin. Beside her walked a tall man
in a dark suit, "That must be Edward," she told herself. Behind
them walked a shorter man, who looked across to David, beside
her, and exchanged a look of greeting with him, "That would be
Matthew," she guessed.

The undertaker's men placed the coffin at the front of the church,
the mourners filed into the pews reserved for them, the minister
took his place and the service began.

Chapter 29
1915

Forget-me-nots

Late July and the beginning of August 1915 was a strange, nothing sort of time. The weather was disappointing. The armies on the Western front were in a stalemate and the flow of men coming home wounded from the war, though it continued, was temporarily reduced. Such action as there was took place away from Europe and largely involved the armies and navies of other nations.

James felt an empty loneliness inside. His male colleagues and friends had gone off to the war, Jacob's return had placed a barrier between him and Mary, Bethan had gone back to Wales for the summer and Win had been transferred to Gallipoli, where there were heavy casualties in the fighting that mainly involved troops from the dominions.

James was glad to get away from Oakdale when the summer holidays started and enjoyed spending time with Win's parents and the boys. The week included a trip to London to see Buckingham Palace and visit the Zoo. The time passed all too quickly, though, and soon James was back in Oakdale again. The boys made several visits to the farm, as they had during the Easter holidays, and James reciprocated by having Hannah, David and Eleanor to visit them at the manse as well. But instead of staying at the farm with the boys, James delivered them there and went back into town to go about his work.

✳✳✳

One morning when Mary came to deliver the children, she pushed past James and headed for the kitchen, saying, with a broad smile across her face,

"I've come bearing gifts. I've baked you some cakes, but I've got something even more special—a bag of flour."

"Thank you very much," James said. He was puzzled as to why Mary would give him flour. The puzzlement showed in his face.

"It's *our* flour, James!" She explained. "From the field we ploughed and sowed together. We sold a couple of cartloads to the miller and I bought back a few bags for ourselves. I thought you'd like to share it!"

A smile broke across his face. "I'll keep it forever," he said.

"That might not be a good idea, she said, It would probably go off!"

"Would you like a cup of coffee before you go back?" he asked.

"Just a quick one," she agreed. They sat, talking and enjoying each other's company while the children went out into the garden to play.

"I've enjoyed chatting to you again," Mary said, as she rose to leave, "I've missed our times together."

"Me too," he agreed. "You know, Mary, it would have been very easy for our friendship to get out of hand. I'm really fond of you and I think you are of me. But I'm glad we haven't got anything to be guilty about. I hope we can always be friends in the same way."

"Friends forever!" she said, "Sounds good to me!"

She kissed him briefly on the cheek, picked up her basket, called to the children, "Eleanor, David, Hannah, I'm going!" and went.

✳✳✳

A week later, James was puzzled by a large envelope that came among his morning post. It wasn't a bill or an official letter of any kind. The handwritten address was in a round, generous, female hand which he felt he recognised.

He opened it to find three letters inside, each in a separate, blue envelope. All three letters were written on notepaper that was printed with little pictures of blue forget-me-nots in each corner.

All three were from Bethan.

One was addressed to "The Chair of the Management Committee, Oakdale Free Church Elementary School". It simply said,

> "I herewith tender my resignation from the posts of headteacher and teacher of Oakdale Free Church Elementary School, with immediate effect."

Another was addressed to Revd Wortley. It said.

> "Dear Rev Wortley,
> Please accept my resignation from the post of Church Secretary. It has been an honour to serve in this position

but I have decided to return to my home in Wales and will no longer be able to fulfil my duties."

The third, simply addressed to "James". said,

"Dearest James,

"I have decided that it will be best for both of us if I leave Oakdale and return home to Wales to stay. I don't want to be a source of difficulty or danger or embarrassment to you and would hate to see your affection for me turn to annoyance, which I fear it would in time if we remained a temptation to each other. I believe it will be best for me to keep away from you and leave you free to fulfil your ministry and be a father to your family and a husband to Win, when she returns.

"I shall not return to Oakdale. I have enclosed two impersonal letters of resignation which you can show to those who need to see them. This is hard for me and I must ask you, please, not to make it more difficult. Please do not reply or try to dissuade me and please do not come looking for me.

"You are the most wonderful man I have ever met and I shall always treasure in my heart the moments I have spent in your company. I will love you forever.

Your

Bethan X X

James felt an almost physical pain as he read the letter. He felt guilt—this young woman's career had been interrupted, hindered, perhaps damaged because of his lack of self discipline. The thought of not seeing her again brought another dimension to the pain. He would miss her. By asking him not to contact or pursue her, was she punishing him? It felt like it. He would have preferred to come to a point where they had a more peaceful closure. Her action seemed sudden and unexpected. He wondered whether there was something she wasn't saying. In part he felt her hurt—he could imagine the agony of feeling love for someone who could not or would not respond.

At the same time, he also felt a sense of relief. His mixed feelings for her had kept him in a state of tension for several months now and she was giving him a way out.

And then finally there was a sinking feeling with the realisation that he would have to report Bethan's resignation to the school management committee and the local education office and he would have to announce her resignation as church secretary to the deacons and then to the congregation. At each stage there would be questions asked to which he could give no satisfactory answer. He would have to initiate the process of finding someone to fill the vacancies, a process which would mean extra work for him and the necessity of stepping into the gap if that process took a long time and responsibilities had to be carried out in the absence of a suitable candidate.

Another thought crossed his mind. What if Bethan were to confide in someone else about her relationship with him? What if the report reached the ears of someone who would not handle it with tact? Was it time now for him to reconsider his position and to step aside, to leave Oakdale and perhaps leave the ministry altogether? He considered making a confession either to the authorities of the two denominations the chapel was affiliated to, or even to the congregation. Rightly or wrongly, he decided against those courses of action. He thought of Joseph in the Bible and his choice not to make a "publick example" of Mary but to "put her away privily".

He felt he could trust Bethan to be discreet. Later on he probably should leave his post as minister of the chapel and possibly even leave the ministry but, before anything, he felt he should make sure that the vacancies left by Bethan's departure were both suitably filled.

Chapter 30
1915

A surprise visit

There's a surprise waiting for you when we get home,"
William said, as he drove out of the station forecourt.
James had just arrived, bringing the boys back to
Millborough for the start of the new term.

"Is it something to eat?" Matthew asked

"Animal, vegetable or mineral?" Edward joined in.

"It's nice enough to eat but you wouldn't be allowed to—and if I
said it was animal I'd get into trouble." William replied.

"Is it a pet?" Edward tried.

"Only in a manner of speaking—and if you happen to come from
Newcastle."

James joined in,

"It sounds as if it could be a person."

"I'm not taking any more questions," William said in a
determined voice. If you guess it, it won't be a surprise, will it?
Just wait and see."

The car turned into the driveway of the house and scrunched to a halt on the gravel. Edward and Matthew raced to the front door, Matthew rattled the letter box and Edward kept ringing the bell. James was still stepping out of the car and had gone to the back to take their cases out of the boot. He still had his head in the boot when he heard the front door open and the two boys both exclaim at the same time,

"Mummy!"

He looked up in surprise and, indeed, there was Win standing in the doorway and giving each of the boys a hug.

"Hello James!" she said. Both of them stood, awkwardly, looking at each other for a full minute. Neither knew quite what to say.

"This is a surprise," James managed, after a while. "Good to see you. You're looking well."

"I arrived only yesterday," she explained, once they had gone in and sat down together in the back parlour. "I only had time to send Mummy and Papa a telegram and that only arrived a few hours before I did. I'm being transferred to a military hospital in Cambridge. I start there next week. They've given me a week's leave, so, here I am."

James had just spent the whole of the summer holidays with the boys. Winifred had not seen them for several months, so it was natural for Win to spend time with them. She quizzed them about what they had been doing during the summer and they talked excitedly about damming up the stream in Oakdale, about fishing for minnows and the games they had played with Mary's children. James held back and left her free to catch up with them. She put the boys to bed and was then able to talk to her parents and James and to tell them about life in the field hospital in France and on board a hospital ship off the Dardanelles.

As the evening wore on, Win began to yawn and to look pale.

"I should be turning in," she said. "I'm feeling so tired."

James began to realise that he would be sharing a bed with his wife for the first time in almost a year. He felt awkward, as they said goodnight to William and Cecilia and went up to the bedroom together. Win's attention had been completely on the children and they had not even exchanged a kiss since he had arrived. The disagreements they had had and the memory of his adultery with Bethan seemed to him to create a huge, tangible and immovable rock between them.

"I've kept a drawer free for you to put your things," Win said, opening a drawer in a chest of drawers."

"Thank you," James said. "It feels strange, sharing a bed together again."

"I know," she agreed. "it's been a long time. We have some catching up to do but I'm really tired. Can we do that tomorrow? I do still love you."

"Understood!" James said

She began to disrobe. He followed suit but turned his back in modesty as he removed his trousers and pulled on his pyjamas. He extinguished the gas lamp and got into bed.

"Good night," he said.

"Good night," she replied and then reached over to kiss him on the cheek."

In the afternoon of the following day, they left the boys with their grandparents and walked along the river.

"We were walking along here almost this same time last year!" Win observed.

"So we were. A lot of water has passed under the bridge since then."

"It has! Last night I told you and Mummy and Papa what's been happening to me." But what's been happening to you?"

James paused. He was about to say, "Nothing." But that wouldn't be true. "It's hard to say…" he began.

He was conscious of the huge rock between them. He felt that, if he attempted to move it, it might crush them both.

"I need to make a confession," he said.

The words were out. He was committed.

Hesitantly, with many pauses and embarrassed silences he began to unburden himself. He explained how his friendship with Mary had blossomed and then how lonely he had felt when Jacob returned. He told her about the flirtations with Bethan and the thunderstorm and how they had gone to bed together. He told her how Bethan had returned to Wales.

"Win, I am so, so sorry." He concluded. I have disgraced myself and dishonoured you." Tears flowed from his eyes and he dabbed them with his handkerchief and blew his nose.

"Have you finished your story?" She said. There were tears in her eyes, too, as she looked into his.

"I have. There's no more to say." James said.

"Alright, now it's my turn," she said.

"I've already apologised for not honouring you. I see the war very differently, having been at the front and seen for my own eyes what it does to people. I'm glad in one way that I enlisted and I'm proud of what I have been able to do. I used to be so selfish. Seeing all that suffering has helped me to find a better perspective on life. By running off, I left you in a more vulnerable position. If I'd stayed,, what you've described might not have happened. And I need to tell you. There was this doctor…"

Win poured out her story, telling how she and Justin, the doctor, had worked together in the field hospital, how she had assisted him with operations, how they had comforted one another and spurred each other on when they were tired and weary—how gestures of understanding and support had turned to caresses—how he had taken her out to a meal when they were on leave—how she had felt a growing love for him—how they had almost given expression to their love and then he had backed off and vowed he wanted to be faithful to his wife. Finally the anguish she had felt when another nurse revealed that he had declared his love to her as well.

"So you see, James, I can understand. Can you forgive me, if I forgive you? We have two lovely boys. Can we make a new start and build a home together for them?"

She took his hand in hers and held it tight. The hours had passed, the sun was going down and a cold breeze blew around them.

"I'm cold," Win said, "shall we go home?" They stood up together, hand in hand.

"Kiss me, James?" Win asked.

They held each other close and their lips met. For a moment they stood, entwined in each other's arms.

"This feels like coming home already." James murmured.

Slowly, they walked back along the river, the sun on their backs and their long shadows stretching ahead of them.

A few days later, Win had to go back on duty at the new military hospital in Cambridge. James stayed long enough to see the boys back to school at the start of the new term. On a visit to the school, he noticed a poster on a noticeboard in the school entrance that advertised a vacancy for someone to teach Greek, Latin and divinity. After some correspondence with Win and discussion with William and Cecilia, he decided to apply.

Chapter 31
1936

Meeting the family

Heulwen had discovered who her father was. In a physical sense, she had located his whereabouts—his body was there at the front of the chapel, in the coffin. But she knew little of him as a person. Everyone else in the chapel had a memory of him. The tears being shed by some of the congregation showed that in many cases the memories were warm and affectionate. The minister who was taking the service spoke of James's achievements, of two pastorates he had held as a minister, of the courage he had displayed at the start of the Great War by speaking out against the conflict. He spoke about the contribution he had made to Millborough School as a teacher. Many of the boys from the school were there in uniform and the school choir sang during the service. Reference was made to a village chapel where he had served as a part time minister while also teaching at the school.

All of this was new to Heulwen. "He was someone I could be proud of," she thought to herself. And yet, there must have been more to it. What happened with Auntie B? Had he forced himself on her? Did she seduce him? Hearing the things that were being said about him she could understand how Auntie B could have been hooked. And knowing how determined her Aunt could be, she knew she would not have stopped until she got what she wanted.

Or was it more mutual? Had her Aunt and this principled, respected pillar of the community fallen for each other? Had they shared a sense of fun? She knew Auntie B had one. When her eyes met his, had there been an answering twinkle?"

And then there were those two young men seated in the front row with their mother. They were apparently her half brothers. What were they like?

✳✳✳

At the end of the service everyone who had come to the funeral was invited to a tea in the hall behind the chapel. The mourners went off to accompany the deceased to the burial.

Heulwen found this part of the occasion the most difficult. People were mingling and greeting one another but she knew no-one, other than David and his family—and most of them she had only just met. She felt exposed and vulnerable. She put her arm through David's and stayed close to him.

After 20 minutes or so, the mourners arrived back. As soon as he stepped into the hall, Matthew spotted David and made a beeline for him, reaching out his hand to greet him.

"David, it's great to see you old fellow! Thank you for coming."

He shook David's hand warmly and then turned to greet the rest of the family, kissing Mary on the cheek and embracing Hannah and Eleanor as if they were cousins. He turned to Heulwen and she began to wish the floor would open and swallow her up. Looking into his brown eyes was almost like looking at herself in the mirror. There was an obvious likeness. He was about to say something and David quickly butted in,

"Meet my fiancée, this is Miss Heulwen Hughes. We've only recently become engaged."

"Well, congratulations!" Matthew exclaimed. "David is one of the finest fellows I know. You're very fortunate to have won his heart,"

"I'm very pleased to meet you." Heulwen blushed slightly as she spoke.

"You're obviously from Wales," Matthew commented, "How did you two meet?"

"I was in Oakdale on holiday," she said. David added. "She was tracing the footsteps of her favourite Aunt. Do you remember Miss Jones, who taught us at the school?"

"How could I forget her? She was the best teacher I ever had" Matthew exclaimed.

"Well she and Heulwen are related."

"Never! And now you're engaged! That's incredible."

At that moment Mrs Wortley came over. She greeted Mary first, with a warm embrace.

"We're both widows now," she said.

"You'll miss him." Mary replied.

It was almost as if Mary and Win were clinging to each other. They shared something no-one else in the room shared with them. Neither could speak about it to each other or anyone else but they each understood.

Edward came up and joined them. Again there was a round of introductions and greetings.

"Allow me to present my new fiancée, Heulwen," David said, "Heulwen, this is Mrs Wortley and Matthew's brother, Edward."

Again, Heulwen said "I'm pleased to meet you." She continued, "I'm sorry it's on such a sad occasion. I'm sad that I never met Rev Wortley. He sounds to have been a wonderful man." A tear began to well up in her eye.

Matthew began to speak. "David's just been telling me that Heulwen is related to Miss Jones who used to teach us all at the school in Oakdale." He said.

For the briefest of moments a slightly shocked and puzzled look crept across Win's face. Then she said, "Really! How amazing. How did you meet?"

"Heulwen was visiting Oakdale on holiday," David explained again. "She was wanting to find out more about Miss Jones and to see where she used to teach."

The conversation moved on to polite enquiries about other members of the two families. Win and Edward and Matthew turned away to greet other guests and mourners. Heulwen didn't notice it but, for the rest of the afternoon, Win kept glancing across the room at her.

Eventually, a moment came when Heulwen was on her own for a moment. Edward was deeply engaged in conversation with Matthew and with Hannah and Eleanor and some other friends from Oakdale who had come down for the funeral. Mary was deep in conversation with a farming family she had met. David was answering a call of nature. Heulwen sat at in a corner of the room, not really knowing what to do with herself.

Win slipped quickly across the room and sat down at Heulwen's side.

"I'm so glad to meet you my dear," she said. "I'm very interested that you know Bethan Jones. She was a colleague of my husband's in several ways. The two of them had quite a lot to do with each other. She was Church Secretary as well as being headmistress of the Free Church school." She paused and then added, "What relation did you say you were to her?"

The direct question hit Heulwen like a football landing in her solar plexus. She had to be truthful.

"Well, I grew up knowing her as my Auntie. We called her Auntie B," she began. "But she died earlier this year. After she died, my Mam and Dad revealed to me that the lady I thought was Auntie B was really my Mam and that they were actually my Aunt and Uncle. Apparently when she got pregnant with me, Auntie B wasn't married. Tom and Louise—her sister and brother-in-law—hadn't been able to have children, so they adopted me so she could carry on teaching and so I wouldn't grow up with the shame of being born out of wedlock."

"Do you mind me asking how old you are? Win asked.

"I'm 20." Heulwen replied.

"Forgive me for prying, but do you know who your real father was?"

Heulwen froze, her face bright red, a look of embarrassment and fear in her eyes." She was trapped.

"We found a letter among her belongings," she said.

"And was it from someone called James?" Win asked.

Heulwen nodded, speechless. Win took Heulwen's hand, lifted it to her lips and then held it in her lap.

"My James confessed to me, back in 1915." Win said. "About an affair he had with Bethan Jones. She ended it and went off to Wales very suddenly and never came back. He didn't pursue her. But I've often wondered if perhaps there might have been a child."

Heulwen was shaking with embarrassment and fear.

"Don't be afraid my dear", Mrs Wortley continued. "I can see James in you. I can see Bethan, too. I don't bear you any ill will. In fact it feels as if James has come back to me in you. Your presence is a comfort. I'm glad you are here, I really am." Tears started to stream down Heulwen's face. Win began to cry too. "Let me give you a hug," she said.

"Are you alright?" Heulwen heard David's voice behind her. She turned and looked at him, her eyes smiling through the tears. "I'm fine," she said.

"'I've just been getting to know my new stepdaughter." Win said. "Heulwen, we must keep in touch. "I always wanted a daughter but God never granted my wish. I know you've already been adopted, but could I 'adopt' you too? And, David, I'm so pleased to have you marrying into our family."

Chapter 32
1915 and beyond

Departure

The Christmas carol service in 1915 was James's last service as minister of Union chapel. Once again, the strains of "Once in Royal David's City" echoed around the building. This time, it was another schoolboy's turn to sing the solo. David read one of the lessons, the one that came just before the sermon. From Luke, chapter 2, he read about Simeon, the old man who welcomed Mary and Joseph to the temple, took the baby Jesus into his arms to bless him and said,

> "Lord, now lettest thou thy servant depart in peace, according to thy word
> For mine eyes have seen thy salvation, which thou hast prepared before the face of all people
> A light to lighten the gentiles and the glory of thy people Israel."

As David returned to join his family in their pew, James rose to deliver his last sermon as minister of Union Chapel.

"Sometimes in life," he began, "we can reach a point where something we are expecting hasn't happened and yet we can see that it is on its way. God promised Simeon that he wouldn't die

until he had seen the Lord's Messiah, the Christ. I wonder how
Simeon imagined that? Perhaps he imagined a grown man, in
armour, with powerful weapons and an army of followers.
Perhaps he imagined the Messiah seated on a throne, dispensing
judgement and bringing peace to the world through his wise and
compassionate reign?

"In the end, all he saw was a baby. But it was enough. He could
depart in peace because he had met the Christ child. The Messiah
had come. The rest was assured.

"I wonder what you are hoping for tonight? Peace on earth? The
return of your loved ones from the front? Mr or Mrs Right—the
person you will spend your life with? Perhaps you are feeling
disappointed and sad because what you hoped for hasn't
happened. Like Simeon you have waited and waited and what you
are waiting for doesn't seem to be coming.

"What God does give you, tonight, is the same gift he gave
Simeon and the shepherds and the wise men. A Saviour. You can
depart in peace tonight. You can go home happy, because you
have a Saviour. Your sins can be forgiven, your future in heaven
can be secured. Peace on Earth seems but a dream, a fairy tale.
But Jesus will bring peace on earth. It may be years or centuries in
coming but it is assured and, in Jesus, we have seen the start
of it.

"When I came to Oakdale three years ago, I expected to stay for a
long time. I had plans and ideas for the chapel. But then the war
came and things have not turned out as I expected. I am sad to be
leaving you. God's calling me to a different task now, that of
bringing up young men to follow and serve him. In Oakdale I
have pursued the vision of peace on earth. I hope to be pursuing
the same vision as I devote myself to inspiring young men with a
love of peace. I know the Prince of Peace. That means I can depart

in peace tonight and so can you. I shall miss you all. I commit you all into God's safe keeping."

There was a tear in his eye as he announced the final hymn, "Hark the Herald Angels sing." He looked around and noticed that several other people were having difficulty in singing because of the emotion they felt, notably Mary, who was weeping uncontrollably, comforted by Jacob.

"We shall miss you Pastor," Jacob said, shaking him warmly by the hand as they left.

"O James!" was all Mary could manage as she buried her face in his shoulder and then reached up to kiss him on the cheek."

"Thank you for all you've done to help us," Jacob added.

"No. Thank you both for the love and support you've given me," James interrupted. "You've a special place in my affections and I shall keep in touch with you. If nothing else, I gather that David and Matthew have agreed to be pen friends and we shall hear of each other through them.

"Now Jacob, it's time for me to turn the tables and ask you to look after this wonderful lady you're married to as you asked me to look after her while you were away. Treat her well and don't go off travelling the world again!"

"Don't worry, I'll take good care of her," Jacob promised.

✳✳✳

A few months before, James had been invited to take up the teaching post at Millborough School. He had found a house for he and the boys to live in, within walking distance of Cecilia and William's home. Win's new posting at the new military hospital in Cambridge seemed secure and Cambridge was near enough for Win to come home when she had time off.

Albert Whale, the former head of Oakdale Elementary School, as it came to be known, was unfortunately killed in action in the Autumn of 1915. The school management committee was able to recruit a new head, a young man who was a qualified teacher and who had not been fit enough to be enlisted in the armed forces.

James had arranged for the carol service to also be his farewell service from the chapel. There had been a wonderful farewell tea in the school hall during the afternoon with a presentation. The next day the removal men were coming to pack up his belongings and to remove them to his new home. In January he would be starting in his new role at Millborough.

The war continued for a further three years after James left Oakdale. The chapel remained without a minister for a year but eventually called an enthusiastic Irishman, the Reverend Walter McEvoy.

There were further fatalities and casualties among the young men of the town. 137 names were carved into the war memorial that was erected after the war.

Soon after the end of the war, Win took up a civilian nursing post at the hospital in Millborough. David and Matthew continued to correspond over the years.

A couple of years after taking up the post at Millborough School, James was also invited to be the part time pastor of a small chapel in a village five miles from the town. He continued to fulfil both responsibilities conscientiously and to good effect until he became ill in 1936.

Chapter 33
1937

A summer wedding

"I call upon these persons here present to witness that I, David Jacob Hollinshead, do take thee, Heulwen Mair Hughes, as my lawful wedded wife, to have and to hold, from this day forward, for better for worse, for richer for poorer, in sickness and in health, to love, honour and obey, until death us do part, according to God's holy ordinance; and thereto I plight thee my troth."

David's voice echoed around Oakdale Union Chapel as he repeated the words phrase by phrase after the minister. The chapel was crowded. Relatives, friends and well wishers had gathered from Wales, from Oakdale, from Millborough and elsewhere.

Deciding where to hold the wedding had not been easy. Heulwen would have loved it to have been in Wales—in Hebron chapel, where she had attended since she was a little girl but, in the end, they decided that the building was too small to accommodate all the guests they wanted to invite. So they decided to get married in Oakdale.

Heulwen looked radiant, wearing a cloche-style veil edged with scalloped lace and carrying a huge cascade bouquet of pink roses. As promised, Awena was her chief bridesmaid. She was accompanied by Eleanor and they were both dressed in high wasted, eau-de-nil, chiffon dresses with puffed sleeved bolero jackets and they each wore a pink silk floral headband that reflected the bride's bouquet and their own, smaller pink rose bouquets.

To compensate for the wedding not being in Wales, David and Heulwen had decided that the service would be bilingual. Reverend Morgan from Hebron had been invited to come and help and he led Heulwen through her response. Her voice trembled slightly with emotion as she too repeated after him, phrase by phrase:

> *"Yr ydwyf fi Heulwen Mair Hughes yn dy gymmeryd di David Jacob Hollinshead. yn wr prïod i mi, i gadw a chynnal, o'r dydd hwn allan, er gwell, er gwaeth, er cyfoethoccach, er tlottach, yn glaf ac yn iach, i'th garu, i th fawrhâu, ac i ufuddhâu i ti, hyd pan y'n gwahano angau, yn ol glân ordinhâd Duw; ac ar hynny yr ydwyf yn rhoddi i ti fy nghred."*

A beam of sunlight shone through he window of the chapel and across their hands as they exchanged rings and Reverend Morgan pronounced them husband and wife, first in Welsh and then in English. Mary, seated on one side of the chapel, looked across to Win and Louise, seated together on the other. All three of them had taken out handkerchieves to blot away their tears.

David and Heulwen walked out to the strains of Mendelsohn's Wedding March as the service came to an end. Photographs were taken outside the front of the chapel and the guests repaired to the Red Lion for more photographs and the reception.

"Doesn't Heulwen look beautiful?" Mary exclaimed as she

greeted the Louise and Win, at the reception.

Louise nodded in agreement. "It's a shame that my sister, Bethan, isn't here to see her. I hope she's lookin' down from heaven,"

"They make a wonderful couple," commented Win. "James would have been so proud of her. He always wanted a daughter but we just had the two boys."

"I feel as if this wedding has healed a wound," she added. "I used to feel jealous when James wrote about how he used to come and help you at the farm, Mary—and I have to confess that Bethan Jones wasn't my favourite person at all. I always felt she had her eye on James—and my feelings for her weren't charitable at all when James first told me about what happened between them. But look at us now—we're all family, aren't we? All the different strands—the Wortleys and the Hollinsheads, the Jones's and Hughes's—they've all come together in these two lovely young people who are making a new start together."

Later in the evening, the guests thronged the platform at the station to wave David and Heulwen off as they left for a honeymoon in the Lake District. David and Heulwen leaned out of the door and waved. A swirl of steam rose from between the carriages, enveloping the crowd of wellwishers. Doors banged. A whistle blew. And the train began to move. In response to a request and a tip from Matthew and Edward, the station master had placed a row of signal detonators on the line, which exploded with a series of loud bangs as the locomotive rolled over them. The guests cheered and waved as the train chugged away into the tunnel at the north end of the station.

Chapter 34
September 1938

Making peace

A little over a year later, Heulwen lay in bed in the nursing home, cradling her newborn baby in her arms. David sat beside her at one side of the bed, Mary on the other.

"We've had a load of telegrams," David said, taking a bundle from a briefcase. "Louise and Tom are coming down from Wales tomorrow. Win is coming up from Millborough on Monday with Edward and Matthew."

"Have you decided on a name?" Mary asked.

"Not quite. We've been thinking about it," Heulwen said. "We thought we'd call him James, in honour of my real father. We thought of David, but he probably wouldn't want the same name as his Dad. We are trying to think of a second name, something a bit special."

A radio stood in the corner of the ward. Music and voices came from it intermittently, too indistinct for them to hear as it was turned down low. At that moment someone turned it up. They paused and listened to the voice of Mr Neville Chamberlain, the Prime Minister,

> *"My good friends, for the second time in our history, a British Prime Minister has returned from Germany bringing peace with honour. I believe it is peace for our time. We thank you from the bottom of our hearts. Go home and get a nice quiet sleep."*

"I've had an idea," Heulwen said. "James Makepeace Hollinshead—doesn't that have a ring about it?"

"I've never heard of anyone called Makepeace before," Mary observed.

"There was a famous writer called William Makepeace Thackeray." Heulwen explained. "I had to study one of his novels at college. Mr Chamberlain's just been talking about peace for our time. And I think our little James has brought peace in a way— he's brought harmony out of his Granddad's troubled relationships. And he's half English and half Welsh, so he unites two nations with a troubled history.

"In that case, he ought to have a Welsh name as well as an English one." Mary suggested.

"Dafydd!" Heulwen said. "That's the Welsh for David."

"James Dafydd Makepeace Hollinshead," David said, savouring each syllable as he pronounced the names.

"That's a name and a half!" Mary exclaimed. "With a name like that, he shall have to be someone really important."

"Yes, I like it", Heulwen agreed.

And that's how he was introduced to the admiring friends and relatives who came to see him in the following days – and how he was named when he was taken to Oakdale chapel to be blessed.

***

The peace that Mr Chamberlain declared proved to be shortlived. By the time James Dafydd Makepeace was trying to stand on his feet, Europe was engulfed in another World War and he was seven by the time it ended.

David worked the family farm for several years and eventually went into politics and became the member of parliament for Oakdale. After bringing up little James and then a sister, Bethan Mary, Heulwen put her teacher's training to use and taught at the very same school where her mother had been headmistress.

Today

Postscript

So, that's the story of my mother and my grandfather, as truthfully as I can tell it. I've pieced it together from what members of my family told me, though I've had to use my imagination here and there. I'm proud to be descended from people with such independence of spirit, from people who loved peace and lived to help others, from people with passion and love in their hearts. People who were imperfect but kept trying.

And that's why I'm called Bethan. I never got married myself. There was someone I gave myself to, when the Beatles were famous, in the late 1960s when everyone was taken in by the "free love" myth. We had sex under the stars in the local park after going to see *A Hard Day's Night* at the local cinema. He was about to move with his family to live in Scotland. Eric, he was called. He moved away and we lost contact. I often wonder what happened to him. He left me with a son, though he never knew it. We called him Jacob, after my Granddad, but he was always called "Jake" for short. We stayed here at Sandybrook Farm with my brother and my Mum and Dad. Jake runs the farm nowadays. I do what I can to help, but I'm an old lady and I can't do what I used to.

Life has some funny twists and turns. The important thing is never to give up. You never know what's round the corner. It's like a relay race. You take the baton from those who've gone before you and, whatever kind of start they've given you, you do the best you can to make it better for those who come after.

Anyway, thanks for taking the time to read this. I hope you enjoyed my story.

Bethan Mary Hollinshead.

If you enjoyed *Poppies and Forget-me-nots*, you may also enjoy other works by Michael Jobling:

Fiction
Encounters on a Bus
The lives of the characters all funnel through the same bus journey in this collection of short stories which build into a kind of a novel, but one that moves sideways through space, rather than forward through time.
ISBN 978-0-9565818-1-5

The Last Bauble on the Tree (illustrated by Naomi Owolabi).
A story for twelfth night.
There's no way that Belinda the Bauble is going to spend the whole year in a box in the loft. When the decorations are taken down she hides and is taken with the tree to the recycling centre.
ISBN 978-0-9565818-3-9

Devotional and Biblical Studies
The Heart of Christmas
Prepare yourself for a Christmas full of meaning.
ISBN 978-0-9565818-0-8

First Things First
A fresh look at the first eleven chapters of the Bible.
ISBN 978-0-9565818-2-2

Jesus and the Brood of Vipers
Why did the most godly people on earth plot to kill Jesus?
ISBN 978-0-9565818-4-6

You can purchase copies of all the above titles to order from the self-publishing website, www.lulu.com